Second Sleep

Also by Diane Stanley

Joplin, Wishing

The Chosen Prince

The Princess of Cortova

The Cup and the Crown

The Silver Bowl

Bella at Midnight

Saving Sky

The Mysterious Matter of the Allbright Academy

The Mysterious Matter of I. M. Fine

A Time Apart

TANLEY

Second Sleep

Quill Tree Books
An Imprint of HarperCollinsPublishers

Quill Tree Books is an imprint of HarperCollins Publishers.

Second Sleep

For information address HarperCollins Children's Books,
a division of HarperCollins Publishers,
195 Broadway, New York, NY 10007.
www.harpercollinschildrens.com

Library of Congress Cataloging-in-Publication Data

Names: Stanley, Diane, author.
Title: Second sleep / Diane Stanley.
Description: First edition. | New York : Quill Tree Books, an imprint of HarperCollins Publishers, 2021. | Audience: Ages 8–12. | Audience: Grades 4–6. | Summary: When Max and his sister Rose go to visit their grandmother's lakeside vacation home, they soon discover that their nightly sleeps bring them to a timelocked place with kids from all different eras, united by their love of the lake—and Max begins to wonder if they can help him to find his missing mother.
Identifiers: LCCN 2021016696 | ISBN 978-0-06-265803-6 (hardcover)
Subjects: LCSH: Missing persons—Juvenile fiction. | Mothers—Juvenile fiction. | Brothers and sisters—Juvenile fiction. | Grandmothers—Juvenile fiction. | Dreams—Juvenile fiction. | Paranormal fiction. | New York (State)—Juvenile fiction. | CYAC: Missing persons—Fiction. | Supernatural—Fiction. | Mothers—Fiction. | Brothers and sisters—Fiction. | Grandmothers—Fiction. | Dreams—Fiction. | New York (State)—Fiction. | LCGFT: Paranormal fiction.
Classification: LCC PZ7.S7869 Se 2021 | DDC 813.54 [Fic]—dc23
LC record available at https://lccn.loc.gov/2021016696

Typography by Michelle Gengaro-Kokmen and Catherine San Juan
21 22 23 24 25 GV 10 9 8 7 6 5 4 3 2 1

❖

First Edition

In loving memory of my mother,
Fay Grissom Stanley Shulman,
1920–1990

For Viola

The Game

IT WAS ONLY AFTER his mom disappeared that Max started playing the game. He'd downloaded it months before because his friend Orson wouldn't shut up about it. The game was simple, he said, something you played on your tablet, but it was—direct quote here—"truly a thing of beauty." Not your typical eye-candy flashy animation that tries to make a fantasy world look real. This game had, according to Orson, "elegant graphic design." Which he knew Max would appreciate. And which Max was pretty sure he would once he got around to playing it. But at the time he was still obsessed with *Muerte: The Skull.*

Then the mom thing happened, and Max got desperate for something to distract him from the dark thoughts that had roosted in his brain like bats in a cave. What he needed was something easy, a game that wouldn't make him think too hard, and wouldn't stress him out any more than he already was. The beautiful and elegant part was just an added bonus.

Turned out, the game met all these requirements. It was, after all, about pruning trees.

So Max opened it and started playing. And right away he saw what Orson meant about the design. It looked like art—flat graphics, stark and clean, with hard shapes in red, yellow, and black. The electronic soundtrack was soft and serene, kind of Zen, with just a hint of foreboding.

His task was to help trees grow by carefully pruning them with a swipe of his finger, guiding them, urging them to lean toward the light while protecting them from various kinds of danger. If he failed, he could always grow another one and try again. But if he got it right, the trees would burst into bloom, then the petals would fly off into a star-filled sky with a whooshing sound, like wind.

Everything about the game was gorgeous. Max found himself wishing he'd designed it himself. The problem was, it didn't go on in the way it had started. With each new level, the world grew more hostile, with fire and drought, urban sprawl, and the shadows of looming factory buildings, wild winds, and dying soil.

At random times he'd get this tiny blue flower, perched on a ledge somewhere, bright and cheerful, a little spark of hope. But that was just a tease because after a while he stopped seeing the flowers anymore. And the trees, no matter what he did to help them, grew gnarled and ugly.

It crept up on him a little at a time. The anxiety began to build and the tasks got harder, until the heart-stopping moment of the muffled explosion, after which the screen went dark. Then the earth was spinning through space and time, the stars whirling by overhead, until it came to rest on the final scene: a single tree, leafless and bent almost to the ground, alone in the darkness of a ruined planet.

But, no, that couldn't be the ending! Max refused to accept it. So he started pruning tenderly, with infinite care, until slowly, slowly it began to right itself, to stand straight, and to grow slowly, slowly toward the light of the stars. Which was all there was left—the sun was gone.

But the tree never bloomed. Instead, it faded to white, or maybe it was silver, like a ghost tree, terrible and beautiful and unbearably sad.

Max was stunned by that final screen. Because the

sense of loss, the hopelessness, was exactly how he was feeling just then—only without the beautiful graphics and the Zen music.

Yet he didn't delete the game. He started over and played it again, hoping it would be like all the other games he'd ever played—that if he figured out the right tricks and was really smart, eventually he could win. But however many times he played it, the ending was always the same.

So why would he keep playing a game that would always end in tragedy? Because he was addicted to it? Because, no matter how badly things turned out, it was still beautiful? Yes to both.

But it also had something to do with Max's inner hopefulness. Because deep down he refused to accept anything short of a happy ending. And he was determined to keep trying till he got one. In the game, and in his life.

What Max didn't yet know—though he would, in time—was that the "right trick" had never been some secret key or special move. The trick was never giving up.

Chapter One

IT'S AN ORDINARY DAY, like any other. In this case a Tuesday in early August. Max and his sister have just come home from Discovery Camp. Which isn't actually a camp, just a summer enrichment program at their school. They like it, though, and go every year.

In the past their downstairs neighbor Penelope would pick them up in the afternoons—from school or from camp—and stay with them till one of their parents got home. But Max has just turned twelve and is now considered old enough to take charge of Rosie on the subway and at home.

He has mixed feelings about this. Rosie can be a real pain. And if she has a meltdown and he's the one in charge, he'll have to deal with it. On the other hand, it means a significant increase in his allowance. And it's nice to be trusted.

On this particular, ordinary day Max is feeling pretty full of himself. Like he's the third adult in the family now, with all this new authority to swing around. Also, he's pumped about his art class at camp. They'd worked on etchings that day, which was something new and totally cool—scratching images onto a metal plate with a stylus, rubbing ink into the scratches, then wiping off the rest, then putting the plate through a press, where the image is transferred through pressure onto a special kind of soft paper.

He loves the feeling of the stylus in his hand, the little scratches in the metal that will become thin black lines, and the way he has to think backward, because the image will be reversed when it's printed. Max feels this technique is perfectly aligned to the way his brain works. His teacher apparently thinks so too. This very day he said Max was "a natural."

Their dad comes home at the usual time, around six thirty. He asks how their day went, as he always does, usually in the exact same words. They answer, as they always do, that their day was fine. Then Dad says, like it's nothing special, "Mom won't be home for dinner tonight."

This doesn't strike Max as unusual. He doesn't ask why she won't be home, whether she has a patient in crisis at the cancer center, or has gone to a conference, or what. He just opens the kitchen drawer where they keep the take-out menus and flips through them. Later, he won't recall what they ordered, or what he did that night. It's too routine to leave a trace in his memory.

It goes on like that for two more days, by which point, for reasons he can't quite put his finger on, Max has started to feel uneasy. He assumes his mom is doing something work-related. And his dad doesn't seem concerned. But somewhere deep in his consciousness he has the sense that something is *off.*

Her absence has caused a shift in their routines. They've retreated to their separate corners, plugged into their devices, hardly talk to each other anymore. They're like a table that's missing a leg. It no longer functions. Lean on it and it'll tip over. His mom, Max realizes for the first time, is the essential element—the sun to their planets.

Another day passes. It's Friday. They've eaten their latest take-out dinner, pretty much in silence. Now Rosie has plopped herself down in front of the TV, which Dad has chosen to ignore because he's in his bedroom messing with his computer. Max figures that if watching endless hours of TV will keep his sister from whining or acting weird, then hooray. He goes into his room to work on a preparatory drawing for his art class on Monday.

He wants the image to make full use of the cross-hatched lines that are typical of etchings. So he does a night scene with a monster coming through a door. Then he remembers what the teacher said about contrast and negative space and decides he needs a light area to set off all that dark. So he starts over, this time drawing a big, shaggy bear walking on a tightrope with a white sky in the background, silhouettes of tall buildings leaning in on either side.

This feels like a total success. It's going to be awesome.

When the weekend rolls around with still no sign of Mom, no calls, no nothing, Max's feelings shift from quiet unease to hard-core anxiety. At which point he wonders aloud, as they sit over breakfast that Saturday morning, when exactly will Mom be coming home?

"I don't know," Dad says.

Just like that: *I don't know.* He sounds kind of snappish when he says it too. Like he's irritated or angry. Like Max has been constantly pestering him with questions, when in fact it's the first time he's even brought it up. Dad doesn't look at him when he says it either, just gazes down at his yogurt and blueberries. His spoon. The table.

"Where is she, anyway?" Rosie asks, having obviously failed to catch the edge in their father's voice.

"She's gone to help a friend."

He's still staring at his breakfast, so Rosie turns to Max with a puzzled expression. Because even an eight-year-old can figure out that "helping a friend" is not a place, and therefore not an answer to her question.

Max gives her a significant look and subtly lifts a finger to say, *wait*. Rosie receives the message: when Dad leaves for the gym, where he goes every Saturday morning at exactly the same time, they will talk.

"Okay," Rosie says as soon as they hear the faint *ding* of the elevator's arrival on the fourteenth floor. "That was weird."

"Yes, it was. He's either super vague or says he doesn't know. It's like he's hiding something."

"You think they're getting a divorce?" Her voice rises a notch or two, edging dangerously close to the dreaded baby whine. And Max really does not want to deal with a Rosie freak-out right now.

"Don't be ridiculous!" he says.

"Why? Lots of people get divorced."

"I know that. But not them. No way."

"Then maybe he's not telling us because it's something bad. Like she's been kidnapped by the Mafia and Dad can't raise the ransom and they're threatening to kill her if he doesn't pay."

"You watch way too much TV."

She shrugs. "Well, something's wrong."

"Yeah, something definitely is."

Then Max has one of those sudden, head-banging, *what-was-I-thinking?* moments. "This is so stupid!" he says, grabbing his phone. "We should just call her!" He can't imagine why he didn't do it days ago.

So he punches in her number and waits while it rings. Rosie's watching him like a vulture, so he turns his back on her.

"*What?*" she says, when Max has been silent for like three seconds.

"Voicemail." He waits for the beep, then leaves a message. "Mom, will you *please* call me back? Because we'd *really* like to know where you are and when you're coming home and Dad's not telling us anything and it's freaking us out. Okay? *Please?*"

"That should do it," Rosie says, heading back into the

kitchen with her mostly empty orange juice glass.

But Max isn't giving up. If his mother is ignoring her calls because she's *so* busy "helping her friend," he'll keep on calling and texting till she finally answers, just to make it stop. As before, it rings and rings, then goes to voicemail. This time he doesn't leave a message.

"What was that?" Rosie's standing in the kitchen door.

"What was what?"

"That humming sound. Like *hummmm, hummmm, hummmm*."

A tingling starts in his scalp, then runs down his neck and into his back and arms till it ends with a shudder. He knows exactly what that was. The kitchen is right next to Mom and Dad's bedroom and their dresser is up against the common wall. Which is why Rosie heard it.

He gets up and goes into their room.

"What are you doing?" Rosie says, standing right behind him.

"I'm staring at the dresser."

"Yeah, I know. But why?"

"I'm thinking." What he's thinking is that it'll feel kind of gross to open his parents' drawers and go digging around in their underwear. Then he hears the humming sound again, exactly as Rosie described.

"That's it!" she says.

The phone is in the third drawer down, under a tidy pile of nightgowns. He pulls it out and answers before the caller hangs up.

"*Dory?*"

"No, Dad. It's me. I think you need to come home right now."

Dad's breathing hard when he comes in, like he ran all the way from the gym to their apartment, which he probably did. "Are you all right?" he says.

"Not really." Max sends the phone sliding like a hockey puck across the coffee table, knowing his dad will catch it, which he does. Max is angry and he wants to make that abundantly clear.

Dad stares at the familiar phone case with the antique-looking flowers on a cream-colored background. "Where did you find this?"

"In a drawer, hidden under her nightgowns. She turned off the ringer but forgot to change the settings so it wouldn't vibrate."

"What—she *hid* her phone? In a bedroom drawer?"

"That's what I just said."

Dad sags in his chair, head flopped back, and stares at the ceiling in silence.

"Time to tell us the truth, Dad."

"I have been telling you the truth," he snaps, pulling out his own phone and turning it on. "Your mom called on Tuesday, but I was in the subway where there was no service, so she left a message. When I called back, she didn't answer."

"And?"

Reluctantly: "I haven't heard from her since."

"You could have told us that. It was the same as a lie, pretending everything was normal."

"I thought it was at first. Strange, but within the bounds of normalcy. And I didn't want to worry you."

"In what possible way is it 'within the bounds of normalcy'?"

"Okay, Max, why don't you just calm down and listen to what she said before you rush to judgment." He presses play on the voicemail message and holds out the phone so they can hear.

Hi, it's me. I guess you're on your way home. Shoot! And now I have to run and catch a train. But I need to tell you I'll be out of pocket for a while. An old friend's in the middle of a crisis and for some reason he needs my medical expertise. I don't know what it's all about, he was very circumspect, but he said it was complicated and might take a while. So please don't worry if I can't get back to you right away. Okay? Love you.

Oh—there's a lasagna in the freezer. You'll have to microwave it first to thaw it out, then bake it till it's bubbly, maybe half an hour. Bye!

"What's *circumspect*?" Rosie asks.

"Careful. Cautious. She meant that her friend was being secretive, not telling her very much."

"And that didn't creep you out?" Max asks. "I mean, right from the start? That she left that message with, like, *no* information, then basically disappeared?"

"I found it troubling, yes. But to be fair, she didn't have much information to give."

"Yeah, she did. Her old friend's name. And where she was going on the train."

"She was in a rush."

"She managed to mention the lasagna."

"Come on, Max, take a deep breath."

Max looks down at his hands instead, not wanting to meet his father's eyes.

"And to answer your question—yes, it did seem odd, even at the beginning. But it was clearly something Dory felt she needed to do. She didn't sound upset, just hurried. And your mom, as you know, is quite a capable person. I trusted her to handle whatever it was. More to the point, she *specifically* said not to worry if she couldn't check in right away. I was giving it a little more time."

"But you called her this morning," Rosie said.

"I've been calling her every day, quite a few times a day, actually. Now I know why she never answered."

He's swiping her phone with his finger now, searching through the incoming calls. Max leans over to watch as he scrolls through a long list of names and numbers. There are Max's two calls, a whole string of them from Dad, and four or five from their grandmother Mozelle. At last he finds the one he's looking for. On Tuesday at 6:07 p.m.:

No Caller ID

unknown

"Great," he says. "The anonymous friend."

"What about Dr. Sharma? She must know something. Mom would have told her she was going away."

"Actually, she did."

"You called her?"

"No. Dr. Sharma called me. Mom had told her she needed to start her vacation a few days early. Said it was a family emergency, and would she cover her patients? So naturally Dr. Sharma was concerned. She thought someone had died."

"But it wasn't. A family emergency."

"I know that, Rosie, but it was probably simpler than going into all that business about an old friend with a crisis. And here's the thing: When your mom tells me something, I believe it, because she's a good and truthful person. And with her word as the absolute given, I've been adjusting the possible scenarios to meet the mounting evidence. But this business of hiding her phone is the real kicker—there's no explanation for that."

"There is, actually," Max says. "Her friend said not to bring it because he might be traced through her."

"What, by the police? You're suggesting her friend is a criminal?"

"I don't know what he is, Dad, but he's using a burner phone."

Silence hangs heavy around them like dread.

"Well," Dad says, "I'm going to go call Mozelle. She's probably worried too. And she might have some light to shed on the subject of Mom's old friends." With that he goes into his room and shuts the door.

Then, as if on cue, Rosie starts to unwind. Max can feel the freak-out coming. And at that particular moment he Just Cannot Bear It.

So he gets a charger and plugs in Mom's phone, turning on the ringer in case Mom actually *has* been kidnapped and there's a ransom call. Gets Fluffy Rabbit from Rosie's room and thrusts it into her outstretched arms. Pops the *Ponyo* DVD into the player. Then he sits on the floor beside his sister as she stares fixedly at the screen, slipping gradually into the warm, familiar anesthetic bath that is *Ponyo*'s magical world, where danger and fear cannot touch her because she's seen this movie a million times and knows exactly how it ends. Love will overcome the wildest storms and the most powerful sorcery. And everything will be resolved in weird and wonderful ways. Happy ever after.

Finally, when Rosie is glassy-eyed and frozen with attention, Max leaves her to it. Goes to his room, shuts the door, and starts playing his game.

Chapter Two

MOZELLE SHOWS UP a little after two. She's brought an overnight bag, which means she'll be staying over. This comes as a relief to Max. Because Mozelle is the only person who, in the absence of Mom, can act as the fourth leg that will make the family stable again.

She's not her usual cheery self, but she still goes through the motions, dispensing hugs like medicine. Then she settles on the couch, Rosie beside her, as the family gathers around the coffee table and gets down to business.

"So, this guy," Dad says. "We know he's someone from Dory's past—she called him an 'old friend.' But she didn't mention him by name, which she would have done if it was someone I knew. That takes us back before college, when I first came on the scene."

Mozelle nods. She's already figured that out.

"Can you think of anybody from the past who seems at all likely? High school, or a summer job? An old boyfriend, maybe?"

"No. I searched my memory the whole way here and no one really fits. By high school, Dory was part of a solid and ongoing group of friends—and you know them all. They were at your wedding. She would have referred to them by name."

"How about before that? Middle school, elementary school, even—like, they used to play together all the time, then as they got older, they drifted apart. But they still went to the same schools and were aware of each other over the years, in a casual sort of way. Then this guy heard that Dory was a doctor, and since he knew her and he needed someone with medical expertise, he called."

Mozelle shakes her head. "He didn't just stop by the hospital or call asking for advice. He expected her to drop everything, including her job and her family, hop on a train, and go help him with some nameless emergency. That's a huge ask from a kid she used to play with in second grade."

"Yeah," Dad says. "You're right."

"This feels like a real relationship, like they have a history and she genuinely trusts him and cares about him. But I can't think of anyone who fits those parameters. Is there anything else?"

Dad shrugs. "Nothing you don't already know. She hid her phone, the caller was anonymous, and we haven't heard from her since Tuesday. It's just so unlike her."

Mozelle removes her glasses, cleans an invisible spot, then puts them back on. "Not to mention that we were supposed to drive upstate on Monday so she could help me clear out the cabin. It was all planned. She'd arranged to take a week off to do it. If she suddenly had to cancel, you'd think she'd have given me a call."

"Oh, Mozelle, I'm sorry! I completely forgot you guys were doing that. It's just, I've been so distracted."

She waves away his apology. "It's okay. But it does give us a deadline of sorts. It may be that she expects to have things wrapped up and be home in time for the trip. I'm sure she would have called me otherwise."

"She can't call if she doesn't have her phone," Max says.

Dad gives him a tired look. "The world is full of phones, Max. Her mysterious friend has a phone."

"If he hasn't already thrown it into the river."

"Okay, that's enough. You're not helping."

They sit for a while in silence, thinking about a world full of phones and a mother who still hasn't called. Then, as if things weren't bad enough, Rosie starts regressing. That's what Mom calls it when Rosie puts on this pouty baby face, shuffles her feet in a baby walk, and lapses into a fake, annoying, high-pitched baby voice. "I want Mommy," she whimpers. (Also part of the act, the "Mommy" and "Daddy" thing.)

It makes Max want to scream. And if they were alone, just the two of them, he might let himself totally lose it. Instead, while Mozelle takes Rosie in her arms and speaks to her in a soft, soothing voice, he starts *Ponyo* over from the beginning. Then he sits beside her, once again, staring mindlessly at the screen, till the sniffling and whimpering finally stop.

Meanwhile, the grown-ups have retreated to the kitchen for a private conversation. This seems unfair to Max. If he's old enough to manage an eight-year-old on the New York subway, he should be included in whatever it is they're discussing. Then, while Max is still sulking about injustice, Dad passes through the living room, unplugs Mom's phone, slips it into his pocket, and says he's going out for a bit. Wordlessly, Mozelle comes in and plants herself on the couch.

Max quietly gets up off the floor and goes over to sit

beside her. "Where'd he go?" he whispers so Rosie won't hear.

Mozelle gives him a sad look, like she really doesn't want to tell him. Then silently she mouths the word *police*.

Two hours later Dad comes home with a bag of takeout from the Indian place around the corner. He doesn't say anything, just passes through the living room again and sets the food on the kitchen table.

Clearly this is a cover-up, to hide where he's actually been—he's gone to get dinner! But as cover-ups go, it's pathetic. For one thing, they usually call and have the food delivered. For another, picking it up in person does not take two hours.

Mozelle gets up casually and joins him in the kitchen. Max, just as casually, follows in her wake. "What did they say?" he asks. "The police."

Dad looks kind of gray. His voice sounds exhausted. "They don't feel it qualifies as a missing persons case. Because of the message she left, how she specifically said she'd be out of touch for a while, and that we shouldn't worry. It's not like she went out to get bagels one morning and never came back."

"Oh."

"I got some curry."

"Yeah, I see that."

"Also I got that eggplant dish you like and some vegetable samosas. And raita. Are you hungry?"

Max looks at him for a long time. "Not even close," he says.

It's Sunday now, a quiet morning—or as quiet as the city ever gets. Max is on the bed with his tablet on his lap, Zen music floating through earbuds into his brain as he swipes the screen with his finger, surgically lopping off branches. He's trying to prevent his latest tree from touching the burning red orb that will turn it into a glowing coal, after which it will collapse into a heap of ash.

Mozelle is in the living room reading to Rosie. And Dad is at his computer, going through Mom's Outlook contacts for unfamiliar male names. Which is why Max has gotten away with sitting alone in his room for hours, pruning electronic trees. His mom would never have allowed it. She's obsessed with "limiting screen time." And if his dad were his normal self, he wouldn't allow it either.

So it catches Max off guard when he hears the knock on his door. He flips the cover over his tablet and yanks out the earbuds.

"Max? Can you come out, please?"

"Okay," he says, hiding the evidence under his pillow, shuffling over to open the door. "What's up?"

"Family meeting."

Max feels a surge of dread. Apparently it shows on his face.

"Don't worry, it's nothing bad. And we're going out to Noodle Village after."

"After what?"

"The *family meeting*, Max."

"So," Dad says when they've settled themselves in the living room, "your grandmother has a proposal to make. Let me say in advance that I strongly approve. Mozelle, want to take it from there?"

"All right. But first I need to tell you a little story. Or not so much a story as a bit of background. So it'll make sense, and you can fully appreciate—"

"Argggh!" Max pretends to tear out his hair.

She laughs out loud. It's nice for a change—laughter.

"All right, all right! Here it is: I propose we go on a little vacation together." She stops there and makes them wait.

One beat, two beats, three beats . . .

"Can you tell us the story?" Rosie says.

"Why, yes, sweetheart, I'd be happy to."

One beat, two beats . . .

Max knows what she's doing, trying to lighten things up. And even though he can see right through her tactics, they work. He really does feel better.

"So, a long time ago, when your mother was five or six, Marvin and I bought a little log cabin in the woods."

Max has heard his mom mention "the cabin" once or twice. He tries to remember more, but nothing comes.

"Is it an actual, real log cabin?"

"Yes, Rosie, though *actual* and *real* mean much the same thing, which is what we call *redundant*." She might have said more, but Max and Rosie start poking her and screaming in protest. Even Dad is smiling now.

"All right," she says when the ruckus has stopped. "The cabin is on the banks of a creek, near a lake, surrounded by every kind of beauty—tall trees and deep blue sky, the sound of rushing water and the wind in the branches, the smell of sun on the pines. We went there every summer when your mom was growing up. Then, around her senior year in high school, she sort of lost interest. There were all these other things she wanted to do—you know, a summer job, hanging out with her friends. So after that, for many years, it was just Marvin and me. And then, well . . ."

They give her a respectful silence while she shakes it off. The sadness.

"So, anyway. While we were dealing with Marvin's illness, a developer started buying up cabins so he could tear them down and build a new development of lakeside homes. Most everybody jumped at the offer. The compound is old, and his price was fair. But even after Marvin died, I refused to sell our cabin because it held so many wonderful memories. And I hated the thought of some developer tearing it down. But I couldn't honestly see myself going up there alone."

"So what happened?"

"Long story short, I finally caved in. The closing is August fifteenth. Now I have to go up there to dispose of the furniture and bring home anything I want to keep. Which takes me to the point of this story: I'd love for you to see it before it's all gone. It's such a beautiful place. I'm wondering if you would like to come with me."

"When would we leave?"

"Tomorrow."

"But what about *Mom*?" Rosie wails.

"If she gets back in time, she can join us. It'll be crowded, but we can manage. And if she doesn't, then your dad will still be here, doing everything he can to find her. The minute he knows anything, he'll call and let us know."

"Where is it—this cabin?" Max asks.

"Upstate, west of Plattsburgh. On Blackberry Lake."

"What is there to do?"

"Besides clearing out the cabin?"

"Yeah."

"Well, you can go boating, or fishing, or swimming in the lake. There are trails for hiking. We can play board games, read books, gaze at the stars."

"Oh."

"Think of it as camping," Dad says, "only with beds and flush toilets and a roof."

"Have you ever been camping?"

Dad looks down, roughly in the direction of his knees, and grins. "I've *read* about camping. I've *fantasized* about camping. I'm pretty sure I know how to make s'mores."

It's a good moment, the first in a long time.

Chapter Three

ON MONDAY MORNING, having spent the night at Mozelle's little house in New Jersey, they pile into her cherry-red Honda CR-V and head for the wilds of upstate New York. The car is old but well cared for. Max is pretty sure it will get them there.

Rosie's in the rear seat, beside her a backpack full of car-appropriate entertainment—old copies of *National Geographic Kids*, some easy chapter books, a three-dimensional foldout puzzle, an Etch A Sketch, and a collection of minor stuffies. The major stuffie, Fluffy

Rabbit, is currently being held in a death grip by Rosie, who is clearly *not all that sure* about this trip.

Max is up front with Mozelle, his tablet on his lap, his own backpack resting at his feet. The radio is playing NPR news.

Their family has never done road trips. Their life is in the city. And when they do travel, like when they go to San Francisco to visit Dad's parents, they fly. So Max is not entirely prepared for the crushing boredom of sitting for countless hours in a car. He holds off for as long as he can, then cautiously opens his tablet and starts playing his game. He waits for Mozelle to say he's being antisocial, but she doesn't. He briefly wonders why.

After several eons, during which time the dinosaurs could have evolved, roamed the earth, and been wiped out by an asteroid, Mozelle pulls off the highway so they can fill up with gas, use the restrooms, and grab a quick lunch. It's a one-stop-for-everything place, designed for road-trippers like them. The atmosphere is depressing. Lots of turquoise and orange.

Rosie orders a burger and fries. Mozelle gets a chicken salad sandwich. Max chooses the grilled cheese sandwich with a side of onion rings. Then they pick a table and wait for their number to be called.

Max looks around for someplace to charge his tablet, which is down to 41 percent, and they still have a long way to go. But he doesn't see an outlet anywhere. Mozelle's car is too old to have a USB port. And Max doesn't own a car charger. Why would he? Like most of the people in New York, his family does not own a car.

Max excuses himself and wanders through the aisles of the ridiculously huge novelty section looking for a charger he can buy. Shockingly, they don't sell them. Funny signs with stupid sayings on them? Yes. Weird key chains? Check. Decorated dish towels, plaster kittens covered in glitter, ugly wall calendars? Take your pick.

On the off chance that he just didn't look in the right place, he asks the people standing behind the multiple counters—*Do you have car chargers?* You'd think he'd asked where the elephants were.

When Max returns to the table Mozelle and Rosie are already eating. He eyes his sandwich with suspicion. It's very thin, soggy looking, mostly just bread with virtually no cheese. The onion rings look strangely artificial, probably made in a factory and frozen for the restaurant trade. He decides to drown them in salt and ketchup. It helps.

Back on the road again, he tries gazing out the window for a while. There are trees lining both sides of the highway, mile after endless mile of them, all the same kind and same size.

They must have been planted when the highway was built, a whole forest of baby trees back then. And it's nice that they went to all that trouble, because it's way better than looking at billboards and shopping malls and motels. But it's kind of like sitting on a beach watching the waves come in. It's pretty, and it's restful, and it's totally great for about five minutes. Then it's just the same thing, over and over and over, until it's not restful anymore. It makes him want to crawl out of his skin with boredom.

When he can't stand it any longer, he pulls the tablet out of his backpack again, puts in his earbuds, and goes back to his game. He tries not to look at the battery icon. There's nothing he can do about it. So he focuses on growing his trees, avoiding various dangers, and honing his skills.

By the time the game ends, in the exact same depressing way it always does, they've left the highway for a two-lane road and his battery's down to 12 percent. He powers off and puts the tablet away.

"Mozelle?"

"Yes, Max?"

"Why does pruning trees make them grow better?"

She shoots him a quick, curious look. And granted, it *is* a strange question.

"Well, as far as I understand, a tree has only so much food and energy to put into growing. So if you take off the lower branches that aren't producing much and probably aren't as healthy as the upper ones, that energy can go into new growth at the top. Trees in the forest do it naturally. The lower branches just die and break off as the tree grows."

"Makes sense. Thanks."

"Just wondering—have you taken a new interest in gardening?"

This is her idea of a joke. Seeing as how they live in a fourteenth-floor apartment and there isn't so much as a potted plant in the lobby.

"It's just this game I'm playing."

"About pruning trees?"

"Weirdly, yes."

"Interesting."

The radio is off now. Mozelle hasn't been able to find a station she likes. In back, Rosie is blessedly asleep. So Max pulls out his phone and the earbuds. At least he can listen to music while he stares out the window.

Maybe it's the motion and the dappled light, or just the hypnotic sameness of tree-tree-tree-tree, road-road-road-road, but his eyelids droop and his mind starts to drift with the music. He leans against the door, using his hoodie as a pillow. Soon he's sleeping too.

Which is great. It passes the time.

"How much longer?" Rosie asks from the back, waking him up. The baby whine is creeping in again.

"About an hour," Mozelle says. "But we'll stop at Millie's Crossing first to get groceries."

Max rolls down the window a bit. The air is fresh and warm with the sweet smell of growing things. Mozelle was right, he thinks. They did need to get out of the city. They were drowning in misery there and it wasn't doing Mom any good. He feels sorry for his dad, though, at home by himself. He tries not to picture it.

The car slows. There's a cluster of buildings ahead. It doesn't look like much of a town, though there's probably more to it than he can see from the road. Farms and stuff. Houses. Shops. And they just passed a sign that said Millie's Crossing, so this has to be the place.

Max asks Mozelle who Millie was. She says she doesn't know. But there was an old bridge over a narrow river right before the sign, so that explains the "crossing" part. Maybe she was a toll collector.

Two minutes later they turn into a dirt-patch parking lot in front of Arnie's General Store. It's decrepit in a picturesque way, like it was built for a movie set in the olden days. The man behind the counter looks fake-real too, as if he was hired to play an old geezer: long, wild gray hair. Bushy mustache. Overalls.

"Well, Mozelle!" the man says when they come in. "Long time!"

"Too long, Arnie."

"So sorry to hear about Marvin."

"I know. Thanks. Arnie, these are my grandchildren, Rosie and Max."

"Well, hey there. Where's Mom and Dad?"

"It's just us," Mozelle says, sliding right past it. "I have 'em all to myself."

"Lucky you. Got a list?"

She fishes one out of her purse and hands it to Arnie, who goes into a back room and comes out with a couple of cardboard boxes, which they systematically begin to fill with everything on the list. Max wanders around the store, killing time. Rosie starts to whimper.

"What?" he snaps.

"I have to go to the *bathroom*." She delivers this in what people call a "stage whisper," audible throughout the store, with the added drama of heavily emphasizing the word *bathroom*. Max closes his eyes and groans. He knows he's being a brat, but he really can't help it.

Mozelle takes a key off a hook by the door and hands it to Max. It's tied by a loop of twine to a big strip of wood with TOILET printed on it in crude white letters. "It's around back," she says. "Can you take her, please?"

Well, of course he can. And to be honest, he has to go too. That doesn't stop him from resenting it. "Sure," he says, picturing a 1920s outhouse, smelly and gross. But it turns out to be perfectly normal, like the gas station restrooms they've visited along the way. The toilet flushes. The water in the sink runs clear. There are even paper towels to dry his hands.

By the time they return, Arnie is carrying Mozelle's purchases out to the car—the two boxes plus a big bag of ice. "See you in a couple of days," he says, shutting the hatchback with a solid thump. "You sure left the cleanout till the last minute."

"I know. Sticking it to the man, like the old radical I am."

He laughs. "Don't forget to bring me any books you don't want. I have the feeling yours'll be good 'uns."

"Oh, you can count on that."

A few minutes out of Millie's Crossing, they turn onto a narrow dirt road. It's rutted in places, very rural. Farmland and forest.

"What's with the ice?" Max asks. "Are we giving a party or something?"

"Ha!" she says. "No. It's for the icebox."

"Icebox?"

"To keep our food cold."

Max thinks about that for a minute. "You mean the cabin doesn't have a refrigerator? Or it just doesn't have a freezer?"

"Neither. It only has an icebox."

For a while there's nothing but the rumble of tires as he processes this new information. Then, "Why not?" he finally asks.

"No electricity."

"*What?*" Max practically shouts.

"*What?*" Rosie chimes in. "You didn't tell us that!"

"I know," Mozelle says, clearly amused.

"But how can we charge our phones and stuff?"

"You can't, Max. Besides, there's no cell phone service out there anyway. But before you panic, I rented a satellite phone so we can stay in touch with your dad at all times. If there's any news, he'll call us. And any time you want to talk to him, you can."

"Great," Max says, heavy on the irony.

"Think of it as an adventure," she says.

Chapter Four

MOZELLE STOPS THE CAR halfway up the drive and insists they get out to admire the cabin. It looks impossibly old, like something built by early settlers with nothing but axes, and handsaws, and sheer brute strength. It sits on the land like it belongs there, at peace with the forest that embraces it and the deep, clear sky overhead.

The open space in front of the house is carpeted with fallen leaves, pine needles, and patches of grass here and there, more an extension of the forest than an actual lawn. And the only sounds are the wind in the trees, the occasional call of a bird, and the continuous burble of running water from the creek nearby.

"Isn't it grand?" Mozelle says, as proud as if she'd created it herself.

"It looks like it's been here for two hundred years."

"More like fifty, but I agree. It feels like stepping back in time."

Rosie seems less interested in the cabin than in what might be lurking in the forest. "Are there bears out here?" she wants to know.

"Black bears, yes. But don't worry, they're shy. Say boo and they'll turn tail and run."

"Have you done that?"

"No. I've never actually seen one, just their scat sometimes. And footprints in the mud after it rains. They keep pretty much to themselves. Though let's not encourage them by leaving food on the porch, okay?"

"Okay," Rosie whispers.

Mozelle gets back in the car and drives it around to the rear of the cabin so as not to spoil the illusion that they're living in the nineteenth century. The kids follow on foot.

Max ignores his sister's shuffling steps on the theory that she'll stop if nobody's paying attention. Mozelle gives Rosie the task of holding the back door open while she and Max unload the car, shuttling back and forth carrying boxes and bags into the kitchen.

The inside of the cabin surprises him. He expected the usual Sheetrock walls you'd see in any other house. But except for the partitions that divide the space into various rooms, the walls are just the other side of the same stacked logs that form the house.

"Doesn't the wind blow through the cracks in the winter?"

"I don't know, Max. We've only been here in the summer."

The kitchen isn't very big. Wooden counters, well worn. A single small window over the sink. An old-fashioned stove with a fat black pipe that runs up the wall and out through the ceiling. And a stubby metal cabinet with a lacquered finish the color of cream. Three doors, two small and one large.

"Is that the icebox?"

"Yup. Ice goes in the top left compartment. Meat down below. Everything else in the main section. Nonperishables stay on the counter for now. I'll put them in a bowl."

"What's a nonperishable?"

She cocks her head, like surely he should be able to figure that out.

"Something that doesn't perish?"

"Come on, Max, use your head. Would bad things happen to a potato if you left it out on the counter for a week?"

"No."

"How about hamburger?"

"Thanks, Mozelle. I think I've got it now."

His attention has shifted to the large soapstone sink with its old-fashioned faucet. "Please tell me there's running water."

She's squatting in front of the icebox, putting stuff away. "Sorry," she says, not looking up. "You'll have to go down to the creek with a bucket."

He stares at her back in silence, mildly aware that his brain isn't functioning all that well, like there's a faulty connection somewhere, or he's getting a lot of static. Mozelle turns then, sees his confusion. "Just kidding, Max! We have a well, a septic system, and a propane-heated water tank. All the comforts of home."

Finished with the icebox, she takes down a large ceramic bowl, pale yellow with a green stripe around the rim. She fills it with the previously mentioned potatoes as well as onions, lemons, tomatoes, and a single zucchini.

"What about the stove?"

"I'm afraid you'll have to chop wood into very small

pieces. First thing every morning."

Max doesn't bite this time. Just waits her out.

"It's propane too."

Rosie has been sitting on the couch all this time, hugging Fluffy Rabbit and working very hard at looking pitiful. So far her efforts have gone unrewarded, so she shuffles into the kitchen making annoying little mewing sounds. "Mozelle?" she says.

"Yes, sweetheart?"

"Can we call Daddy?"

Five minutes later, they're sitting on the porch steps, Mozelle holding the satellite phone. "With this amazing device," she says, "you could call your dad from the top of Mount Everest. Or the jungles of Brazil. Is that not truly awesome?"

They solemnly agree that it is.

"But it runs on a battery, which has to be charged. How would you do that on Mount Everest, I wonder?"

"I have the feeling you're about to tell us," Max says.

"Better—I'm about to show you."

Beside her on the step is a black object that looks like a blood pressure cuff, only larger. She unrolls it to reveal eight plastic strips, two side by side in four rows. "These are miniature solar panels," she says, setting the little array in a patch of sunlight, then hooking it up to the phone. "Now it's charging—see?"

They do.

Max pictures some guy on the top of Mount Everest, encased in down and technical climbing gear, stopping to charge his satellite phone. How would he do that? Drape the solar collector over his shoulder as he trudges through the snow? Set it on a rock when he stops to eat lunch?

Since the phone is already fully charged, Mozelle unplugs it and carries it out into the yard, raising the antenna as she goes. "I'm guessing we'll get better reception out here, away from the trees."

She punches in the number. Max imagines the signal beaming out into space, connecting with a satellite that's orbiting the earth, then pinging back down to his father's cell phone in New York.

And that, to be honest, is the most exciting part of the whole calling-Dad thing. Because, not surprisingly, nothing has changed since they left this morning. No word from Mom, no new information. At least they have proof that the sat phone works.

Since Rosie's the one who insisted on calling, she gets to go first. But phones tend to render her speechless, so her end of the exchange is limited to one- or two-word answers to a string of questions from Dad. "How was the drive?" "What's the cabin like?" "Are you having fun?" (Her answers: "Okay," "It's nice," and "I guess.")

But Rosie seems perfectly satisfied. She's made contact, heard his voice, and verified that Dad is still in existence. Now she hands the phone to Max, who decides to show his sister how it's done.

He describes the cabin, mentions the lack of electricity, and promises to take some pictures before his phone goes totally dead. He enthuses about the wonders of satellite technology, then asks the obligatory, basically pointless question—how is Dad doing? The answer, as expected, is "fine."

A much overused word. He expects he'll be hearing it a lot.

The cabin has only two bedrooms. So Mozelle will share the big bed with Rosie while Max will sleep in his mom's old room. He finds this mildly disturbing, as if part of her, the ghost of her former self, is still there.

He brings in his satchel and backpack, looks around the narrow space: The blue-and-white quilt on the rustic wooden bed. The framed Chagall print on the wall beside the door, picturing a white goat and a person holding a violin, both of them magically floating among the branches of a large blue-and-yellow tree. On top of the dresser there's a line of well-worn paperbacks, held in place by a pair of iron bookends shaped like bulldogs.

Bulldogs—what is *that* about? Mom has never been a dog person, at least not as far as he knows. Maybe they were a gift.

The books are what you'd expect from the daughter of a librarian: *A Wrinkle in Time*, *Black Beauty*, *The Secret Garden*, *Jane Eyre*, *Little Women*, *Anne of Green Gables*, and a few classics like *Treasure Island* and *Robinson Crusoe*. Max has read none of them—though he guesses he'll be reading them now, since there isn't much else to do in a cabin in the woods with no electricity. And he has maybe half an hour left before his tablet shuts down.

Suddenly he's *that* close to crying.

Over a game. Seriously.

But no, that isn't it. It's way bigger than that. It's all of it, everything. And for one brief moment it's almost more than he can bear. He stands in front of his mother's childhood library, frozen, waiting for the feeling to pass. Then, still shaking, he sets his satchel on the bed and opens it.

Mozelle told him to "unpack and settle in." But something in Max resists this. It's a commitment to staying in a place he doesn't want to be, while Dad goes home every night to an empty apartment, endlessly waiting for a call that won't come. They should have stayed in New York.

They should all be together.

Once again, a wave of panic rolls over him. Again he waits for it to subside, wondering if this is how it's going to be from now on, one panic attack after another. He tells his mind to go somewhere else, to focus on the task at hand.

He pulls out the top dresser drawer. Tosses in his underwear and socks, his tablet and phone and the useless charger that goes with them. His jeans and shorts go in the second drawer. When he opens the third to put his T-shirts away, he finds an old-fashioned album, the kind people used to put pictures in. He's almost afraid to open it. More ghosts.

But it's just a collection of old dried flowers and leaves, all of them cocooned in plastic wrap and taped to the pages. Under each one Mom has written the plant's name, first in English and then in Latin, having presumably looked them up in a plant book. It strikes him as a very Mom-like thing to do.

He puts the album back in the drawer, tosses in his T-shirts, then takes his toothbrush into the bathroom and sets it on the side of the sink. Turns on the faucet to verify that there actually is running water. And there is, only it's kind of gross and dirty looking. So he just stands there, watching it run, wondering if that is *really* the water they're supposed to drink and cook their food in—until gradually the yellow fades to clear. That's a relief, anyway. So he turns it off, exits the bathroom, and shuts the door.

And with that, he's done. There's nothing left to do but lie on Mom's old bed and consider the long days and endless nights he'll have to slog through till it's over and he can finally go home.

He wonders how his mother could have loved this place so much. Yet Mozelle has assured them she did.

"Max?" It's Rosie, peeking in through the half-open door.

"Go away."

"Mozelle says we should go check out the creek."

"Fine. Check it out."

Her voice goes up a notch. "I want to do it *together.* Don't be a *toad.*"

"I'll be a toad if I want to." That sounds so stupid it makes him laugh, and laughing makes him feel better. "We might be attacked by bears," he says, just to be mean.

She crosses her arms and tries to look fierce, which is even funnier.

"Okay," Max says. "Waitin' on you."

The creek is shallow and rocky, the water clear and cold. They take off their shoes and wade in, squealing as the current tickles their feet. After a while, Rosie starts gathering smooth stones of roughly equal size, which she carefully lines up on the bank.

"What are you going to do with those?"

"I dunno. Something."

In other words, it's a completely pointless exercise that doesn't need a purpose, since it's weirdly fun just searching for the right stones, comparing them, picking out the best ones.

"Let's pretend we're a prince and princess and we're collecting rocks to build a castle."

Softly, Max groans. He's been groaning a lot lately. "No," he says.

"Why not?"

"Because I have a better idea."

She's interested. She stops rock collecting and waits.

"Okay, so we're a prince and princess and our kingdom—Novo Yorkus—has been enchanted by a wizard. And, just to be extra-super evil, the wizard has stolen every last piece of gold in our entire treasury and turned them all into stones. Then, to be even more evil than extra-super evil, he whisked them away by magic and threw them into this creek."

"Oh no!"

"But! What he doesn't know is that we *also* have

magical powers, so we can tell which are ordinary rocks and which are pieces of gold in disguise. Now we must retrieve the kingdom's fortune so we can we equip ourselves to defeat the wizard. That is our mission."

This is a huge hit with Rosie. Suddenly she's a changed person, happy in her task. She could probably go on hunting rocks forever.

Fortunately, that doesn't happen. Mozelle calls them in to dinner.

By then they're pretty much numb with cold. And when they step onto the bank, their wet feet pick up all manner of crud—mud and pebbles, dead bits of grass. So they fill their shoes with the prizewinning stones and walk barefoot back to the cabin.

Somehow Mozelle has anticipated this. There's a plastic dishpan full of warm water waiting on the bottom step so they can rinse their feet. There's a towel to dry them. And an empty bucket, presumably for their stones.

"I bet Mom used to wade in the creek," Rosie says.

"She probably had a rock collection too."

It's like they're following in her footsteps, doing the same things she did years before. Living in the same cabin, looking out at the same views. Soon Max will sleep in her bed and read her books.

"It almost feels like being with her," he says. "Does that sound weird?" He drapes the towel over the railing to dry.

"Sort of," Rosie says.

"Does it creep you out?"

"No. It's nice."

Max decides it's a little of both.

Chapter Five

MOZELLE HAS HAD A LONG DAY OF DRIVING, so dinner is a bare-bones affair—instant mac and cheese, a salad on the side. They sit at an old pine table set against the left front window, with a view of the trees and an orange evening sky.

Max notes that there are just enough chairs for a family of three. He wonders if that's the magic number now. They were a family of three in the old days when Mozelle and Marvin came there every summer with Mom. There are three of them now. And in the future, back in New York, will they once again be three?

When it gets too dark to see what they're eating, Mozelle brings out one of the battery-powered lanterns. It's annoyingly bright, so she sets it on the floor in a far corner. The ceiling reflects the light and fills the room with odd shadows. Then she brings a candle to the table. The flame flickers like a thing alive.

"What do we do now?" Rosie asks.

"Finish dinner?"

"I mean after."

"Wash the dishes."

She giggles. "After *that.*" Max is eager to hear the answer because he's been wondering the same thing. The options seem pretty slim.

"We could play a board game."

"What do you have?"

"Monopoly, I think. I'll have to look."

"Noooo," Max moans. Rosie joins him.

"Not your favorite?"

"Noooooooo!"

"That's all right. I doubt we have all the pieces anyway. For that matter, I'm not even sure we still have the board. It's been a long time. And to be honest, we usually went to bed after dinner anyway." She checks her watch. "It's almost eight fifteen."

"You can't be serious!" Max says.

"Why not? People have been going to bed with the sun since the beginning of time. This business of lighting our houses and streets at night, staying up till all hours—that's just happened in the last couple of hundred years. It's just a blip on the great arc of history."

"A blip?" Rosie says.

"Hardly anything at all."

"They had candles," Max points out.

"Yes. But unless you were rich and could afford to buy them, you had to make your own. You also had to chop and haul extra firewood to keep the house warm in the evenings—and that was on top of all the work you already had to do, taking care of animals and working a farm. So instead of doing all that work to light their houses and stay warm at night, they just bundled up and went to bed."

"And slept for, what, twelve hours?"

"Longer if it was winter and they lived in the north."

"Nobody can sleep that much."

"Probably not all at once. They'd sleep four or five hours, then get up and do things for a while—say their prayers, maybe light a candle and do some chores. Monks actually had a regular prayer service in the middle of the night. Still do, I believe."

"Then what?"

"Then they'd go back to bed and sleep another four or five hours. They called it their 'first sleep' and 'second sleep.' There's been research on this. It's what the human body does naturally."

"Not this human body."

"That's fine. There are some excellent books in Dory's room. You can take one of the camping lamps, stay up as late as you want." Her face is unreadable. It's hard to tell if she's just tired or if she's annoyed with Max and his complaints. He's been getting that reaction pretty often of late. Maybe he deserves it. When Mozelle starts clearing the dishes, he jumps up to help.

"We can wash up," Rosie says. "We do it at home."

"I know you do, and I wholeheartedly approve."

She leans against a wall and watches as Max scrubs and rinses the plates, the salad bowl, the silverware, and the pot the mac and cheese was cooked in, then passes them on to Rosie to dry. They've been doing this since she was five. She broke a couple of things at first, but nothing after that. She's always very careful.

"You know, I remember something your mom once said."

Rosie sets the third plate on top of the other two. Max puts them away on the shelf. Then he finds a second dish towel and dries the pot while Rosie does the salad bowl.

"She said she dreamed more vividly during her second sleep, and that her dreams were sweeter. I've also found that to be true, though it was different for her somehow. She asked us to put a blackout blind on her bedroom window so the sun wouldn't wake her up too early."

"That's weird. It sounds like a depressed person."

"Max," Mozelle says. "Make an effort, please."

"Sure. Okay."

She kisses his cheek and the top of Rosie's head. "Long day, old bones," she says. "Party on, you two. I'm going to bed."

Max plays the game till his tablet shuts down. This happens in his least favorite world, where he's in a deep, ugly, industrial gutter with old broken machines and strange metal grates. It's such an unfriendly place, you have to grow your trees in three steps. The first two trees are like prisoners in a dungeon who never escape into the light. All they can do is grow tall enough to release a few seeds onto a perilous ledge where a new one can grow. Only the third tree is able to reach the narrow ray of sunshine and grow—just enough to produce a couple of sad little blooms.

He's halfway through the second tree when the screen

goes black. It feels unfinished, but it's also a kind of closure. There will be no more gaming, googling, surfing, or texting until he gets home. For the next week—or however long it's going to be—he'll live like a peasant from the Middle Ages, going to bed when it gets dark. He'll spend his days collecting rocks he has no use for, making up stories to keep Rosie from getting all weird, and worrying about his mom, who might or might not still be alive.

He closes his eyes and lies very still, but there's no way he can possibly sleep. He isn't tired, and the bat cave in his brain is a swarm of activity, cranking out one ghastly scenario after the other. It's a mash-up of every horror film he's ever seen, except that Mom is always the victim and the Old Friend plays a variety of roles from a zombie to a vampire to your garden-variety sadistic killer. Max can feel his body seizing up again, building tension, practically humming with it, like there's enough bad energy surging through him to charge his tablet *and* his phone.

He gets up and walks in circles, does jumping jacks, stares out the window at the darkness, then goes back to bed and turns on the lantern. It blasts out of the darkness like a flashlight in the face, so he drapes a T-shirt over it, which helps. Then he goes over to the dresser and inspects the lineup. Nothing really speaks to him except *Robinson Crusoe* and *Treasure Island*, which are classic adventure stories.

He pretty much knows the plot of *Robinson Crusoe*—a guy is shipwrecked on an island, he sees footprints in the sand, he has a sidekick named Friday, he builds a house out of whatever he finds. Max isn't sure how he knows all this. It's just out there, the way you don't need to actually read *Frankenstein* to know what it's about. Anyway, it sounds a little boring. So he decides on *Treasure Island* instead, since it's about pirates and a search for hidden gold.

It was written a long time ago, so a lot of the words are different from the ones we use today. But he likes the *idea* of the story, and the foreshadowing at the beginning gets him interested right away. Also, there are these really colorful characters. A little cartoonish, maybe—the good guys and the bad guys—but it's exciting and suspenseful. The bats in his mind cave have roosted now, eager to hear what happens next.

When his attention starts to drift and his eyes don't want to stay open anymore, he turns off the lamp and lies as still as he can. He pretends he's an injured soldier fallen on the battlefield, trying desperately not to move because the enemy is searching for survivors to shoot or stab with their bayonets. His only hope is to play dead very convincingly. He practices taking slow, shallow breaths so they won't see that he's breathing.

His mind is entirely focused on breathing. In, out, in, out, in, out.

Hours later he wakes in the silence of the night, feeling rested and fully awake. So he gets up, tiptoes through the living room, and quietly opens the door.

It's surprisingly cool outside, considering that it's August, and he's stunned by the deep and utter darkness. He's not sure where the moon is. Maybe it hasn't risen yet. Or maybe it's just a tiny crescent hidden behind the trees.

He can barely make out the pillars and railings of the porch. He moves cautiously toward them, gets a handhold, and feels his way down the stairs and out into the yard. Then he just stands there, marveling at the blackness of the sky and the brilliance of the stars.

Having spent his whole life in New York, where it's never quiet and never dark, the experience is shockingly beautiful and strange. He sprawls out on the ground so he can gaze at the sky without straining his neck. The ground is lumpy and scratchy under his T-shirt and on his bare legs. He wishes he'd brought a blanket to lie on. Actually, two blankets would be better, the other one to keep him warm. But he toughs it out because the view is worth it.

He tries to find some of the constellations he's seen at the Hayden Planetarium. But there are so many stars it's like static—he can't pick out the patterns. The one thing he's sure of is the Milky Way.

He knows the earth is a part of it, but that seems impossible—it's so distant, just a smear of starlight across the blackness of the sky. Is the earth maybe on the far, far edge of it? Or is there that much distance between each of the other billions and billions of stars in the Milky Way? The mere thought is frightening—the incredible vastness of this tiny, tiny portion of everything else that's out there. And the thought that the universe goes on and on and on, and no one knows where or if it ends.

He's not sure how long he's been out there—long enough that he'll probably have permanent dents in his back from the pebbles and lumps he's been lying on. So he gets up, stiff and cold, and follows the protocol of ancient humans as described by his grandmother: he goes back to his mom's old bed for his second sleep.

Chapter Six

WHEN HE WAKES AGAIN, the stars have gone and the sun is up. Actually, it's been up for quite a while. It feels like mid-morning, maybe ten o'clock, and he can't imagine how he could have slept that late with so much light streaming through the window. Also, how is it possible that no one else is awake? Yet both of these things are true.

He wanders into the living room and finds it empty. No cooking smells are coming from the kitchen. The door to Mozelle's room is shut. It's absolutely dead quiet.

So he goes outside again, sits on the porch steps, looks

around. The air is still fresh from the cool of night, but the hint of a breeze is warm. He relaxes into himself, feeling the sun on his arms, enjoying the rich, piney smell of the trees.

Then, out of the corner of his eye, he catches a glimpse of something that doesn't fit the landscape. It's moving, a bright flash of color. Soon that something turns out to be a girl, walking down the road in his direction.

She hasn't noticed him yet. She's looking up as she walks, gazing around and smiling, enjoying the perfect morning, the trees and the sky. There's something about her expression that strikes him. It's like her inner self has worked its way to the outside, so he can see the things it usually takes a long time to know about a person—that she's smart, and kind, and will make him laugh. He knows all that at first sight.

He gets up and casually strolls out to meet her.

"Hi," he says, hands in pockets, doing his best to look cool. "I'm Max."

This is stunningly unlike his usual self. He is not what you'd call an outgoing person. His social life, if you can call it that, mostly consists of hanging around with a group of brainy nerds like Orson. Max used to have friends who were girls, back when he was younger. Now they're older and the rules have changed. The *girls* have changed. And

Max finds, to his embarrassment, that he's mildly afraid of them. So for him to suddenly burst into flames over some poor, unwitting girl who's simply minding her own business, walking innocently down a dirt road, is beyond all explanation. He's like Max-in-the-sky gazing down at Max-on-the-ground, going, *Who is this person?*

"I'm Lila," the girl says. "And you're new!"

It flickers through Max's mind that if she'd gone first, if she'd said, "You're new," before he'd told her his name, he could have said, "No, I'm Max," and that would have made her laugh. Only she didn't, so he can't.

"Yeah, we got here yesterday," he says instead. Dull, but accurate.

"We did too. I haven't even unpacked."

Her hair, which Max thought at first was red, is really more of a reddish gold, long and wild, and there are freckles sprinkled all across her face like fairy dust. Small as she is, she gives the impression of standing very tall, like she's ready to take on the world.

"Max?" she says. "You're staring."

He's vaguely aware that, in fact, she's been talking. Something about the weather. And there was probably some silence in there, too?

"Sorry," he says, the tips of his ears burning. "It's just that you're so . . ."

"Freckled?"

"Well, yeah, I mean the freckles are great. But I was actually admiring your posture."

She laughs out loud. "My *posture*?"

"Yeah. Shoulders back, head erect. It makes you look—"

"Like a soldier?"

"No, bold. It makes you look bold."

That seems to knock her over. Like it was totally unexpected, but she likes it.

"Wow. I get *petite* a lot because I'm short. And *perky*, which is gross. But I will heretofore announce that no, I am *not* perky. I'm bold!"

"*Heretofore?*" Now it's Max's turn to laugh.

"It means—"

"I know what it means. I just love that you used a word like that."

"Yeah?"

"Yeah. And you know what else? When I first saw you coming down the road, I knew you were going to make me laugh."

"Really? Is detection your superpower?"

"Apparently so."

"Can you detect where I'm going?"

"Hold on," he says, covering his eyes and tilting back

his head as if communing with the spirits. Silently, he counts to four, then makes a flourish with his hand and says: "No."

She punches his arm. It's a cute punch, not hard, but he dances back like she's done major damage. So they giggle like they're six years old. And Max is still watching himself, still astonished, but definitely encouraged now.

"Well, since your powers have failed you, I will reveal the truth," she says. "I was on my way down to the lake to see who's here."

He blinks, confused.

"Want to come?"

They pause at the end of the road, where it curves around a cluster of trees, then suddenly opens onto a panoramic view of Blackberry Lake. The lake is vastly larger than he expected, and glassy smooth, its still surface reflecting the intense blue of the sky. On the other side of the lake is a broad expanse of green with huge outcroppings of granite. And beyond that, in the far distance, low mountains, soft in the morning haze.

"Wow," he says.

"I know. We go over there in the boats sometimes. It's one of my favorite places."

Below them is a large area that's clear of trees. In the

center is a grassy field where an informal game of kickball is going on. To the right, away from the lake and hugging the forest's edge, is a playground busy with squealing children. Below the playground is a fire circle with two rings of logs around it, currently empty, and four picnic tables, one occupied. A pier juts out into the lake, with three rowboats tied up and waiting. A group of sunbathers are stretched out on towels.

Max can make no sense of this. Mozelle had said they were the only ones there, the last to clear out their cabin. The developer will be starting work in a matter of weeks. Yet there must be thirty, thirty-five kids down there. So where did they come from? Maybe there's a second development, like Cabins I and Cabins II, and only Cabins I is being torn down?

"Can you swim?" Lila asks, taking his arm and leading him down the slope.

"Of course."

"Good. The water's really clear, fed by mountain streams. It's cold, though."

"I can take it. I'm tough."

"How about fishing?"

"A firm no on that one. I'm vegetarian."

"You don't have to eat them. It's catch and release."

"That's almost worse. You're torturing the fish."

"*Torturing?*"

"Seriously, think about it from the fish's point of view: a hook in the mouth, a near-death experience, just so some human can have a bit of fun."

"I see your point. Come on."

Lila is aiming for the occupied picnic table, where an older girl and a younger one are playing chess. A tall boy seems to be offering advice while two kids on the opposite bench are watching the game.

The older chess player spots them and waves energetically. "Lila!" she calls. "Whoop! Whoop!" The younger girl turns, then starts waving and shouting too.

"Omigod," Max says. "That's my sister!"

"Cute! She plays chess?"

"Apparently she does now."

Rosie comes running over, stops in front of them, jumps up and down. "Isn't this cool?"

"Definitely," Max says. "But how did you get here ahead of me?"

"I woke up and everybody was asleep. Then I saw Dee and she asked if I wanted to come, so I did."

"Dee?"

"She's over there."

This is the older chess player, slim and tan, with long, dark hair so perfectly straight, it looks like she must have ironed it. Someone told him about that once, that girls literally ironed their hair back in the hippie days. He'd tried to picture it—leaning over an ironing board, unable to see what you were doing, yet somehow managing not to burn yourself or set your hair on fire.

"She and Lenny are teaching me how to play chess. It's hard, though."

"Well, yeah. But who knows, maybe you'll turn out to be a prodigy."

"What's that?"

"A person who's shockingly good at something at a very young age. Like Mozart. Or Bobby Fischer."

"I don't think I'm one of those."

"Don't worry, most of us aren't. Lila, this is my sister, Rosie."

"Max and Rosie—your mom must be a teacher."

"A doctor, actually." Max says it really fast, before Rosie can get in a word.

"Cool. I just thought, you know, they're both names from Maurice Sendak. Max from *Where the Wild Things Are* and Rosie from *Really Rosie.*"

"Our grandmother was a librarian."

"Well, there you go, Rosie Real. No star shines as bright as you." And when Rosie looks confused: "It's from the lyrics. To the show. *Really Rosie.*"

"Oh." Not quite getting it but pleased to be the brightest star, she skips off toward the picnic table, Max and Lila following.

"People," Lila announces, "this is Max, Rosie's brother. Max, this is Dee, your sister's new best friend." She blows two-handed air kisses at Dee across the table. "And this is Lenny, who isn't tall enough already, so he has to perch on the table and loom over everyone instead of sitting on the bench like a normal person."

"I am the god of chess, Lila. I'm expected to loom. Hello, Max."

"And these two are Amber and Zach."

"A to Z," Max says off the top of his head.

"Yeah," Amber says, deadpan. "It's why we're friends." They slide over to make room for two more on the bench. Dee goes back to studying the board, then moves her bishop.

"Aha!" Lenny says, beaming at Rosie. "*That* is what we call a blunder! Now look at the board. Do you see a golden opportunity?"

Rosie grows as solemn as church. Pinches her lips together. Wrinkles her brow.

"You might consider—"

"No, don't! I want to do it myself."

"Good for you. Go for it."

They're all a little breathless now, waiting in silence as Rosie thinks it through. Everyone, Dee included, wants her to succeed. So when Rosie gasps and moves her knight to take Dee's bishop, everyone claps and cheers. Rosie's so proud that Max is afraid she might burst into tears. And suddenly he just loves these people, loves the warmth of their circle, their humor and kindness. They're like the kind of friends you'd invent in a fantasy.

"Your move, Dee," Lenny says.

That's when the soccer ball comes flying in like a comet out of the sky, slamming into the table, barely missing Lenny's head and scattering chess pieces everywhere. Rosie shrieks, then begins to wail as a tall girl comes racing by, calling, "Sorry, sorry, sorry!" as she heads off the ball before it rolls down the slope and into the lake. Once she has it, she circles back and joins the others on hands and knees, gathering up the scattered pieces.

"I was almost *winning*!"

"It's okay, Rosie," Dee says. "Lenny will put everything back exactly the way it was. Then we can finish the game."

"He can't remember where they were!"

"Actually, I can," Lenny says, adding two pawns and a knight to the jumble already on the table, then spreading them out for a quick survey. "We're missing a black rook and a white pawn."

When the last two pieces are found, they watch, spellbound, as Lenny returns each one to its former position.

"He's a genius," Zach explains to Max. "He has a photographic memory."

"Actually," Lenny says, "I do not. Because there's no such thing. It's just a matter of paying attention. Go ahead, Dee, your move."

All eyes shift back to the players as Dee brings out a rook.

"Oops," Lenny says, giving Rosie a wicked smile. Another golden opportunity.

It goes on in this way, with Rosie working out all her own moves, while Dee makes mistakes on purpose and Lenny gives Rosie all the time she needs. Max finds this incredibly touching.

And yet. Glaciers move faster than this game of chess. A person could grow old and die just waiting for it to end. So when Amber and Zach decide to go join the kickball game, he and Lila excuse themselves too.

They walk down toward the lake, then onto the pier where the teens hang out—or, to be more precise, lie side by side on towels, baking in the sun like a small pod of seals. It's a challenge getting past them without treading on random body parts.

He and Lila sit at the end of the pier, their legs hanging over the edge. The view is still spectacular, but subtly different now that a light breeze has ruffled the surface of the lake. Tiny wavelets catch the light and sparkle like diamonds.

"Isn't it gorgeous?" she says.

"Yeah. On a scale of one to ten, I'd give it a twelve. No, fourteen."

"Every year I come back and it amazes me all over again."

"Surely it's not always like this."

"Pretty much, yeah."

He tries to imagine this being true. He can't quite go there. But it makes him think of San Francisco. Maybe it's sort of like that.

"You know about microclimates?" he asks.

"No."

"Well, in San Francisco, where my grandparents live, different neighborhoods have different weather. I mean *way* different. So in the Presidio it'll be cool and windy but downtown it'll be hot. Some places are foggy and some are sunny. So maybe this is a microclimate too. One where the weather's always perfect."

"Glad to have a scientific explanation," she says. "I'd

always figured it was done by magic." She shoots him a *just kidding!* grin. He shoots a grin back. He's thinking that Lila, like the weather, is almost impossibly perfect, when the silence is broken by a scream.

They whip around to see Rosie running in circles and waving her arms. Only now does he remember that he's supposed to be looking after her. Which he hasn't been doing. He's left her in the care of a perfect stranger—who, granted, turns out to be a very nice and responsible person, but still. And now she's screaming hysterically while he's busy hanging around with Lila, admiring the view and discussing microclimates.

He's up in an instant, speed-walking back down the pier, weaving his way through the pod of teens, past the boats tied up to the pilings, then onto the beach and the grassy edge of the playing field.

Closer now, Max sees that Rosie has not been injured, threatened by a bear, or bitten by a rabid racoon. She's taking a victory lap.

He slows to a stop. Lila catches up. "I guess Rosie won," she says.

"Yeah. She'll be impossible to live with now."

"Nah, it'll give her confidence. That's a good thing."

Max has never given a thought to Rosie's confidence. But as the youngest person in the family, she has to be super aware of all the stuff she can't do that the rest of them can. And there are special rules just for her because she can't be trusted to look after herself. No wonder she acts like a baby.

So, yeah, Lila's probably right. To master a new skill, then win at a hard game you've never played before—that would be a huge confidence booster for sure.

And with this thought his mind is drawn to the playground, where other kids Rosie's age—and some much younger, five or six years old—are scrambling over the play equipment and squealing and chasing one another in circles . . . without a single grown-up there to watch them.

Actually, there's not a single grown-up anywhere in sight.

"Where are all the parents?" he asks.

"Um. Back at their cabins?"

He stares at her, incredulous. She looks embarrassed, like this is somehow her fault.

"You don't find that disturbing? I mean, what if one of those little kids fell off a swing and got a concussion?"

"I know that's how it looks. But trust me, they're not in danger. You'll understand soon, I promise."

"How can you possibly know that? And how am I supposed to 'trust you' when you don't explain anything, and what you do say doesn't make any sense? You'd never see kids that young alone on a playground in New York."

"This isn't New York. Things are different here."

"That's *not* helpful, Lila."

She's close to tears now. "Max, please, can we finish this tomorrow? Then maybe you'll understand?"

That stops him cold. "Why would tomorrow be any different?"

"Because you'll know more then."

"About what?"

"You'll see."

This is so deeply unsatisfactory and disappointing that Max is relieved when Rosie comes running over to tell them, in a very loud voice, what they already know.

"I won, I won, I won!"

"That's great," he says, his voice flat.

"I can't wait to tell Mozelle!"

"I'm sure she'll be very—" And then he stops, horrified.

"What?" Lila says.

"I didn't tell my grandmother where I was going. Didn't leave a note or anything. If she wakes up and finds us gone, she'll freak out." He is sick with self-loathing now. What a total screw-up!

"I promise, it'll be okay."

This makes him want to scream. If she says "trust

me" or "I promise" one more time, he's going to totally lose it. So he turns to Rosie instead. "Did you tell Mozelle you were coming here?"

She shakes her head.

"Then we have to go. *Now!*"

"I'll see you tomorrow?" Lila says, like it's a question. But Max is already walking away from her, practically dragging his sister along. He can't stop picturing Mozelle, panicked and tearful, searching for them, going down to the creek, then up along the road—calling, calling, calling their names.

He's gripping Rosie's hand too tight. "You're hurting me!" she says.

"Walk faster, then," he says.

Chapter Seven

HE OPENS HIS EYES TO an unfamiliar ceiling in an unfamiliar room. It takes a while for the fog to clear and for Max to remember where he is. When he does, he continues to lie there, unmoving, awash in disappointment, disgust, and despair.

The three Ds—his new normal.

Because *of course* it wasn't real! That couldn't have been more obvious if there'd been a neon sign at the end of the pier flashing THIS IS A DREAM, STUPID! A pathetic case of Wishful Thinking While Asleep—the perfect girl, the instant friends, Rosie's triumph, the Technicolor landscape.

And if he'd stayed for the rest of it, instead of running off (or waking up), his mom would surely have appeared, bright and cheery and fine, fine, fine. Followed no doubt by some unicorns and an official-looking person with one of those giant cardboard checks announcing that Max had just been awarded ten million dollars for being such an awesome human being.

Thus, the tone of his waking thoughts. Not a great way to start the day.

Mozelle is sitting at the pine table with a cup of coffee and a book. She looks up at him and smiles. "Sleep well?"

He can't bring himself to answer, just nods.

"There are muffins in the oven. Help yourself. There's cereal too. And orange juice."

Wordlessly, he goes to the kitchen, then carries his breakfast to the table. He eats mechanically, chewing, swallowing. Stares out the window because he can't deal with people right now. He's still too raw.

Rosie comes out of the bedroom holding Fluffy Rabbit by the ear, her hair the usual morning mess. This isn't the fictional Rosie Real, the Brightest Star who made all her own moves the first time she played chess. It's the old, familiar Rosie, who crosses the room with small, deliberate steps, like a toddler just mastering the art of walking, her lower lip rolled forward in a baby pout.

"Can we call Daddy?" she says, her voice an octave higher than normal.

Calling Daddy is her new solution for everything.

"Of course," Mozelle says. "But let's have breakfast first. There are muffins in the oven. Use a hot pad and be careful not to burn yourself."

Rosie shuffles off to the kitchen and solemnly returns with a little muffin on a big dinner plate. It's so comical and sweet, Max almost cracks a smile.

Mozelle sips her coffee, turns a page. Rosie picks minuscule bits off her muffin and eats them one by one.

"I went out to look at the stars last night," Max says, giving his voice a try. "I'm pretty sure I saw the Milky Way."

"Yes. I saw it too. I go out every night when I'm here unless it's raining. There are so few places left in the world where the skies are truly dark."

Rosie gazes thoughtfully at her muffin, as if she'd asked it a question and is waiting for the answer. "Mozelle?" she says to the muffin. "Do you have any other games—besides Monopoly, I mean? Chess, maybe?"

Max turns to her and stares.

"We had an old checkerboard that your mom repurposed for chess. She made her own playing pieces out of clay. But they were completely different from the usual ones—dragons and bears, things like that. She knew what each animal represented, but I could never keep them straight. Had to keep asking her, 'Now, this is a bishop, right?'"

"How old was she?"

"Eleven, I think. Maybe twelve."

"Do you still have them?" Rosie asks.

"No. They fell apart years ago. It was a shame—they were so cute."

"Rosie," Max says. "After we finish the dishes and talk to Dad, want to go down to the lake and check it out?"

It's still early-morning cool as he and Rosie head off together. The air is absolutely still, as if it's holding its breath in suspense.

The light comes in at an angle, casting long shadows that dive across the road. Which isn't the way it was in his dream. It was warm, no shadows. The air even had a different smell, like the sun had woken the forest.

Yet in every other way it's the same. The road, as it turns first left, then right, wandering through the forest instead of cutting straight through. The same kinds of rocks are embedded in the dirt, cool gray against the reddish brown of the road. The ruts he and Lila avoided are there. And that final turn where the whole landscape of lake and mountains is suddenly revealed—he sees it again now, just as it was in his dream.

His mind has trouble accepting this. Because it isn't possible to dream a place you've never seen before. And not just in a general way, but specifically, down to the smallest detail—the pier, the picnic tables, the field, the playground, the fire ring. The vastness of the lake, the parkland across the water, the misty mountains.

Rosie runs ahead, straight for the picnic table. She plops herself down in the exact spot where she sat beside Dee playing chess. She folds her arms, leans forward, chin resting on her right wrist. "Do you think they went home for breakfast? Do you think if we wait, they'll come back?"

Max stares at her. He needs to sit down. "I don't know what to think," he says.

She fidgets, kicking her legs under the table, humming to herself. She's restless but prepared to wait.

Max looks around the clearing more carefully now and sees that it's not *quite* the same. Or, rather, it's the same place but an older, run-down, neglected version. No boats are tied up at the pier. The tables are spotted with lichen and mold. The logs around the fire circle are rotting into the ground. And there are no swings on the swing set, just the metal frame from which, at some point, for unknown reasons, they were removed.

Also, the place is empty.

"Rosie," he says, "I want to go."

"But what if they come back and we're not here?"

"That's not going to happen."

"How do you know?"

"I just do. Come on, this is depressing."

She doesn't argue. Simply gets up and follows him back up the slope to the road, not skipping ahead anymore. Silent, in her own world.

"They'll be here tomorrow," she says.

He's walking more slowly now, not looking ahead but at the grassy verge, searching for breaks in the trees. He knows there must be other cabins here, yet they walked all the way down to the lake without seeing a single one. But of course, he wasn't looking for them either. And the cabins are probably hidden behind the trees. So the best way to find them would be to follow the driveways—or the overgrown remains of what *used* to be driveways once upon a time.

Basically, Max is gathering evidence. He hopes that,

once he has enough information, the things that seem so confusing now will suddenly make sense. Only, he can't quite imagine how that could happen. Because neither of the two competing realities holds up to close inspection. Yet, weirdly, both are supported by his own personal experience.

He can only come up with one theory that would explain it all: that he is delusional. Like people who think they're Napoleon. Or believe they've been abducted by aliens.

He doesn't *feel* delusional, though. And what about Rosie? Could he and his sister both be suffering from an identical delusion? Surely not.

He's found an open space now, grassy and overgrown but wide enough to be a driveway. It runs straight for a bit, then curves to the left and disappears behind the trees.

"Come on," he says to Rosie. "I want to see what's down there."

"Why?"

"Just because."

They trudge through knee-high scrubby grass till the path turns and a cabin is revealed. It's just like theirs, only bigger. Also, it looks abandoned. The windows are coated with years of grime; the paint on the trim has peeled away. There are spiderwebs everywhere. The yard has run wild with weeds and the forest is encroaching. A few saplings have already taken root.

"It looks haunted," Rosie says.

"Yeah, it does, kinda. Want to go around back?"

She clearly does not. But she'd rather stick with Max than be left alone, so she walks close beside him—on the far side, away from the cabin—holding tight to his arm.

"You know there's no such thing as ghosts, right?"

"Okay."

"It's just an old house. That's all it is."

"Okay." But she doesn't let go.

The back is worse than the front. A rusted-out charcoal grill lies on its side, half buried in the tall grass. There's an old clothesline, the rope rotted and split. Trash is scattered everywhere—mummified rags, soda cans, the remains of a bag that once held charcoal—all of it wadded and decaying in the weeds.

"I don't like it here," Rosie says.

He goes to the nearest window and peers through a film of dirt into an empty room. The owners must have sold the cabin long ago. Max can think of lots of reasons why—they were getting old, their kids had grown up and moved on. Or maybe they needed the money. What he can't understand is why they left it in such a mess.

They must have loved the place once. Come here every

summer, year after year. Had cookouts, hung their bathing suits and towels on the line to dry in the sun, spent evenings sitting around the fire circle with their family and their summer friends. You'd think they'd have bothered to pick up the trash, if only out of respect for those good memories. Like properly burying the dead.

"Max?" He can hear the urgency in her voice.

"What?"

"I want to go home."

He wonders whether she means the cabin or their New York apartment. Probably both.

He drops Rosie off at Mozelle's, then continues up the road in the direction Lila came from when he first saw her in his dream. Her cabin shouldn't be hard to find. There's not much green space between Mozelle's property and the entrance to the compound. Just enough, he figures, for a single house.

The driveway, when he finds it, is as wild and weedy as the other one. He follows it anyway, to another abandoned cabin. This doesn't really come as a surprise. And it supports the obvious version of the truth: that no one else is living in the compound except them, what Max experienced was just a dream, Lila and her friends exist only in his mind, and none of those things ever happened.

But. The "dream" hasn't faded the way normal dreams do. It's still as clear in his memory as the drive from New York, the visit to Arnie's store, and rock collecting with Rosie at the creek. Not only is it clear, but it flows and feels like reality, with none of that nonsensical stuff you get in regular dreams—the teacher who at some point morphs into a dog, but then drops out of the story entirely, and for some reason you find yourself in a movie theater, only nobody else is there and you can't figure out where the exit is . . .

And then there's the biggest problem, the one Max keeps going back to: He accurately "dreamed," down to the finest detail, a real place that he'd never seen before. And Rosie "dreamed" it too—the same location, events, people. Even the chess game.

So that's the problem in a nutshell. Both versions have glaring flaws. And in one way or another, both are impossible. So with nothing resolved in the Department of Making Sense of Things, Max's mind wanders to a new thought: *How can I get into that house?*

He's pretty sure the front door would be locked. Besides, some of the boards on the porch look sketchy, and he's not eager to find out the hard way whether they'll hold his weight or not. So he goes around back. Finds a toolshed there, its door ajar by a couple of inches. Over time the shed has sagged to the right. Now the door is wedged into the dirt and weeds. As far as Max can see into the darkness, there are nothing but cobwebs inside.

The kitchen door is locked. He pulls at it anyway, thinking maybe it's just stuck, but it still doesn't budge. So he goes around trying the windows, hoping at least one of them was shut but the latch not turned. That would be such an easy mistake—you lock the doors but forget about the windows.

The third one he tries moves a little. Not latched, then—though the wood has swollen with damp, so he really has to put his back into it. After about five minutes he's opened a space just wide enough for him to slither through like a snake. It'll have to do.

He lands on the floor of an empty room, then wanders around taking stock. It's a two-bedroom cabin, same layout as Mozelle's. But all the furniture is gone. The icebox is empty, the shelves bare. There are no towels in the bathroom. No books on the bookshelf.

He returns to the smaller bedroom to shut the window—he'll exit through the back door like a normal person. That will mean leaving it unlocked, but the house is going to be torn down anyway. He doesn't suppose it matters now.

That's when he notices for the first time that the space is slightly different from his mom's old room, which doesn't have a closet, just a wall of horizontal logs facing the bed. Apparently, the family that owned this cabin hired someone to build one, adding a Sheetrocked section that sticks out a couple of feet, with a door in the middle. The rest of the wall, to the right of the closet, is the same as in his room. They had a dresser there, or a desk. He can tell by the dents in the floor.

There's nothing in the closet, just a wooden rod, no hangers, and the usual shelf above the rod. He sweeps his hand along it and catches nothing but cobwebs and dust. He wipes his hand on his jeans. The spiderwebs are sticky.

He stands there for a while, listening to the quiet. The place feels hollow, empty in a different way from just not having furniture or or rugs or pictures on the walls. Even the echoes of the people who lived in that house, their breath, their essence, have gone forever.

Looking down, he catches a faint reflection from the closet floor, over in a corner. He reaches down and picks it up. It's a hair elastic, the kind girls use instead of regular rubber bands to hold their ponytails together. Where the two ends of the elastic meet is a blue ball with facets meant to look like a precious stone, though it's actually just plastic. Something you'd buy at the drugstore.

He takes it to the window, holds it to the light in the palm of his hand. And there, caught under the fake jewel, is a single strand of red-gold hair. He closes his eyes and concentrates on breathing. This is Lila's hair, it has to be—an actual sample of her DNA, not in a dream but in the waking world. The real, flesh-and-blood Lila wore that elastic at some time in the past. Lost it, forgot about it. Which means she slept in that very room in the now-empty cabin. Hung her clothes in that closet. Looked out that window—and when they left for good, forgot to lock it.

Where, he wonders, is she now?

Mozelle is standing on a dining chair, taking down books from the upper shelf. She's made up two of the boxes they bought at Office Depot in New Jersey and has labeled them with a fat marker. One says KEEP and the other, DONATE. The rest of the boxes, still just flat expanses of cardboard, lean against a wall, waiting their turn. On the coffee table is a jumble of books whose fate has yet to be determined.

Rosie's on the floor in front of the toy box, half its contents scattered around her. *Scraps of our mother's childhood*, he thinks, not for the first time. The scraps are everywhere.

The keepers have been gathered into neat little piles,

small islands of order in a sea of clutter. There are a lot of Legos, the plain ones from the olden days when they didn't come with figures or anything extra. A few random puzzle pieces. A set of building blocks, the wooden kind for little kids with bright-colored letters on them. A handful of jacks with no ball. And, best of all, the tiny, silvery tokens from the old Monopoly set—a shoe, a top hat, a thimble, and a Scottie dog.

"Max!" Mozelle says, stepping down from the chair in that slow, careful way older people do potentially dangerous things. "I found something you're going to like."

She takes a book off one of the coffee table piles and hands it to him. It's bound in cloth, a soft, dusty pink with a strip of sage-green fabric running up the spine. But there's no title on the front. No lettering at all.

"What's this?"

"Dory's book of plants."

"Oh, right. There's an album of dried plants in my room."

"I know. That was her first effort. But we didn't have the right materials for pressing flowers, or the knowledge either, so they tended to fall apart when they dried. She tried protecting them with plastic wrap and that just made them look ugly."

"Yeah," he says. His thoughts exactly.

"So the next year she decided to draw them instead, using the colored pencils we gave her for her birthday. I think she did a marvelous job, don't you?"

He opens it to a carefully hand-printed title page, just like in a regular book:

The Plants of Blackberry Lake

by Dorothea Glickman

Blackberry Lake Press
New York

After that, it's page after page of nature drawings, mostly flowers and leaves, a few acorns and pine cones. Just like in the scrapbook, she wrote their common and Latin names below each one. But the pictures themselves are astonishing, painstakingly drawn and full of little details, like a ladybug crawling on a leaf.

"I didn't know Mom was an artist!"

"Oh, yes. She had a very fine hand, and the patience for careful work."

He carries the book to the couch and settles there,

slowly turning the pages. The more he looks at her pictures, the more he wants to do drawings like that himself.

"Do you still have the colored pencils?"

"Probably. They'd be in the toy box. You can look. Actually, you could help Rosie clean it out for me. See if there's anything worth keeping."

"Okay," he says, still turning pages. He thinks about the time it must have taken her to do even one of those pictures. And there are so many! His mom must have spent her whole vacation doing nothing but drawing. Yet he can tell, just by looking at her work, how much she enjoyed it.

Toward the end of the book, she moved from copying real plants to inventing new ones. She did them with the same care as all the others, had even given them funny made-up names.

There's the *Sunburnus spikeulus*, a fat red ball perched on a stem with sharp little spikes instead of petals. And the *Weepum worryum maximus*, a drooping bell-shaped flower weeping small tears onto the grass below. She drew little shadows along the edges of the tears and added a tiny reflected light where it bulged, the way Max had learned to draw a sphere in art class.

"This is so amazing!"

"Yes," Mozelle says. "It made me think of you."

* * *

Dad calls again after dinner that night. He still has nothing new to say. He's just gotten home from work, hasn't eaten, sounds exhausted.

Max tells him all about Mom's book and what an amazing artist she was. He says he found her old colored pencils when they cleaned out the toy box, and Mozelle is pretty sure she can get him the same kind of blank journal at Arnie's General Store. Max has lots more to say—how he wants to make a book of his own, though his won't be about plants—but it's clear that Dad is only half listening. Like he doesn't even have the energy to manage a simple conversation. So Max says good night. And then, "I love you."

He can't remember the last time he said that. It just isn't something his family does. Not that they don't love each other or show affection, they're just not that direct. With them it's more hugs and cheek kisses, hair stroking, little jokes.

But tonight it feels right. Necessary even. He hears it in Dad's voice when he says, "I love you too, Max"—something that sounds like gratitude. Max feels it rising in his chest then—the emotion he's been trying so hard to tamp down. Now it washes over him, a warmth that brings comfort, but sadness too. Because his father must be so lonely, there by himself.

And, well . . . Mom.

Not long after that, he goes to bed. By the light of his T-shirt-covered camp lamp, he reads more of *Treasure Island*, which is definitely growing on him. By the time Billy Bones is dead and Jim has found the treasure map in his sea chest, Max is all in. He will read it to the end, then move on to *Robinson Crusoe*.

At last he turns off the light and lies very still, just as he did the night before but without the wounded soldier thing. He just concentrates on steady breathing and relaxing his muscles, systematically, one after the other. He isn't sleepy, just worn down from carrying around so many feelings and struggling with things he can't understand.

His mind really needs a break.

He doesn't know what will happen when he finally sleeps (then has his time with the stars, then sleeps again). But just in case, he's lowered the blackout blinds.

Chapter Eight

LILA IS WAITING AT the foot of their driveway. In her blue-and-white sundress, with her hair flowing crazily down her back, she looks like a model in a shampoo commercial. The romantic kind, soft focus, flowy dress, standing in a field of flowers.

Just to be sure, he touches her arm.

"I'm real," she says.

"Just checking. I'm very confused."

"I know. It's easier when you're little. I was like five or six my first time. At that age, you don't try to make sense of it. You just kind of go with the flow."

"Yeah. Rosie didn't question anything. She just wanted to know when the people were coming back."

"Sweet." She takes his arm, pulls him along. "But you're past all that now? The struggle, the mind bending?"

"Not entirely—though you were right about my grandmother. She wasn't worried about us because we'd never actually left the cabin. We were still there, sound asleep."

"True."

"Same with the kids on the playground. They were safe at home with their parents."

"Right. You've got it, then."

"I wish. The thing is, I went to your cabin yesterday. It was empty—no furniture, no people, no nothing. And I'm pretty sure it was your cabin, because I went inside and I found this." He produces the elastic band with the strand of red-gold hair. "I'm guessing this is yours?"

She holds it in the palm of her hand, staring at it thoughtfully for a while, then looks back up at Max. "Yeah. I loved these when I was Rosie's age. They came in ten-packs with plastic jewels in all the different colors." She hands it back. "You can keep it if you want."

He does want. He slips it carefully back in his pocket.

"So, since we've now established that I had the right

place, I have to ask where you are *right now*. Where are you sleeping and dreaming from? Because it's definitely not that deserted cabin."

She sighs. "Actually, it is."

"That's not possible. There isn't even a bed."

"Max, it's deserted in *your* 'now.' But my 'now' is different."

"What does that even mean? And different how?"

She sighs again. "Different as in 1983—okay? I'm guessing your 'now' is somewhat later."

"*Somewhat!* It's 2019."

He does the math. In her "now," the moment in time she's dreaming from, Lila is his age. But in his "now," she's old enough to be his mother. Something sharp and sour rises in his throat, and for a moment he thinks he's going to puke. But he swallows hard a couple of times and his stomach finally settles.

"That's the sort of information we're not supposed to share," she says. "So this is kind of breaking the rules."

"There are *rules*?"

"Not written down or anything. We just all agree that it's better if we don't talk about our other life or try to, you know, *connect* with each other outside the compound. You can see why. We just keep it all in the collective 'now.'"

"The '*collective now*'?"

"Yeah. Lenny came up with that, if you haven't guessed. I kind of like it."

"Okay," he says, still struggling to piece this thing together. "Just to be clear, you're saying that you, and your friends, and all the other kids are each dreaming from different times, different 'nows.' Yet somehow we all manage to come together in the same dream? Which Lenny calls—"

"The collective now. Yes."

"But only here?"

"Yes."

"And you're how old, in your 'now,' in 1983?"

"I'll be thirteen in November."

"I don't know how to feel about this. A little sick, maybe."

"Really? I've always thought the dreams were wonderful and magical."

He remembers her little joke about microclimates and the weather, that she was glad to have a scientific theory to explain it because she'd always thought it was done by magic. She'd said "just kidding" then. But apparently, she wasn't. Now she's asking him to believe it.

"Well, okay," he says. "Let's pretend this is true. And yeah, it is pretty amazing. But it's just so . . ." He can't think of the word. Finally he settles on "limited."

"How do you mean?"

"Well, let's say I met you—and Lenny and Dee and Amber and Zach—at an airport. And we hung out together and we really hit it off. We just instantly felt like friends, the kind of friends you want to keep. But then our flights are called and we're all going different places, so we won't ever get to see each other again. That kind of limited. Hello, goodbye."

"No, Max! We'll see each other again tomorrow, and the next day, and the day after that, and it'll go on like that through most of August. Then we'll go home, back to our own time, but next summer we'll all meet up again, a year older but with plenty of time left. I know it's not forever. But we won't start ageing out for a long time yet."

"What does that mean?"

"Well, you remember how yesterday you noticed there weren't any grownups around? That's because we stop dreaming around sixteen or seventeen. Like the kids on the pier—they're ageing out. Most of them won't be back next year."

"Is that why they just lie there in the sun like they're half asleep?"

"Yeah. I guess. Probably. But my point is, we have a lot of years ahead. It's not 'hello, goodbye.'"

"Sorry, but you're wrong. That may be how it is for

you and the others—which is great. But for Rosie and me, it's not a matter of years or even weeks. It's a matter of days."

She gives him this fierce look, like she's mad at him for saying that, never mind that it's true.

"And after that, we can't come back. Not ever."

She stares at him, appalled.

"The thing is, it's not just your cabin that's empty in my time. All of them are except ours. They've been sold to a developer who's going to tear them down and build a bunch of fancy new lakeside homes."

"No!"

"Yes. We're the last ones to leave. We only came up here so my grandmother could clear out the cabin. Then we go back to New York. And that's it, end of story."

"When do you leave?"

"A few days, I'm not exactly sure."

"And can't come back?"

"The *developer*, Lila? What I just *said*? The tearing-down-all-the-cabins thing? What would I come back to—a construction site? But it won't affect you, I promise. You'll still get to have all of those years. You'll be aged out and grown up before any of this happens."

"But it *will* affect me because you won't be here." She's looking down at her feet now, like she's trying not to cry.

"Okay, so this is kind of embarrassing, but I need to tell you something. When I woke up yesterday and realized you weren't real, just some fantasy I'd made up in a dream—well, it was really crushing. I mean *awful*! Because I like you a lot. I liked you right from the start."

"Me too. I mean, I like *you* a lot. Not me."

"Got it, Lila. So, I'm thinking—since, you know, my plane will be leaving really soon and all that—maybe we should make the most of the time we have. Because after I leave, all I'll have left of our time together will be memories, and I don't want them to just be 'the funny girl with the cool freckles and bold posture.' I want to actually know you as a person. But we could start with stuff like, what's your name and where do you live?"

"Lila Marie Kelly. From Rochester."

"Thank you. I'm Max Sotelo from Manhattan, no middle name."

"Now what?"

"I don't know—you tell me stuff about you and I'll tell you stuff about me. We'll see what happens."

"Okay. I know this really beautiful place we can go. It's kind of far, but we can talk on the way, then talk when we get there. Anything you want to know, anything you want to tell—we'll break all the rules. Sound like a plan?"

It does.

* * *

They leave the road and head into the forest, staying close to the edge. Looking out, they can see the playing field, where a somewhat more organized ball game is in progress. The children on the playground are doing what little kids do. The pod of ageing-out teens are still baking on the pier. And their friends are splashing in the water down by the boulder field. But Max and Lila are hidden in the deep shade, surrounded by trees.

"If we head off to the right and go straight through the forest, we can cut the corner and get there faster. Okay with you?"

"That's cool. I've never actually been in a forest before. I remember when I was a little kid how all the fairy tales and nursery rhymes were about things and places I'd never experienced—farms and forests mostly."

"Castles and milkmaids."

"Yeah. But 'the woods' were dark and dangerous. A place where wolves hung around looking to hit on little girls in red capes. And all those lurking witches bearing grudges."

"Well, I can't speak for the witches, but I'm pretty sure we're safe from wolves."

"What about bears? I hear they're shy."

"I've heard that too. Watch your feet. You don't want

to trip over a root or step in a rabbit hole."

Max dutifully watches his feet. Deep in the forest the ground is more uneven than where they were before. And the sound of their footsteps is more pronounced—twigs crack, dried leaves crunch. If there are any wild creatures nearby, they will not be taken by surprise.

"Want me to start?" Lila says, her voice low, as if she doesn't want to disturb the forest any more than they already have.

"Sure. Go ahead."

"All right. So, if you haven't already guessed, with a name like Kelly, we're Irish. My great-great-great-grandfather—I think that's the right number of greats—came here sometime in the 1840s. He was just a kid, nineteen or twenty, with no education. But he was young and strong, so he could always get work doing construction. But he never learned a trade, so he stayed on the bottom rung of the ladder his whole life. He married an Irish girl who washed dishes in restaurant kitchens. They had a bunch of kids and they were always poor. But it got better in the next generation."

"How do you know all that? I mean, the 1840s—wow!"

"The Irish are famous storytellers. And our stories got passed down."

"That's so awesome."

"Also, he could sing. It's what everyone always remembered about him, his beautiful voice. Your turn."

"Okay. But first I need to ask a question. Do you live in a regular house—you know, with an upstairs and a downstairs, and a yard with grass and trees, and a car in the garage?"

"Yes. Two cars, actually."

"Well, we live in an apartment on the fourteenth floor of a great big building. We don't know most of our neighbors. Technically it's a three-bedroom apartment. But that's only because the people who owned it before us divided one of the bedrooms into two. So you can imagine the shape—long and thin, like a very large coffin with a window on one end and a door on the other."

"Hmm."

"Yeah. So then there's the living room, kinda small, and the kitchen. One bathroom. To go outside, we ride down in an elevator and walk out through a revolving door. And the outside is mostly sidewalks and streets, lots of traffic, a few trees. We walk most places we go, but if it's too far or the weather's bad, we take the subway. And we don't have a car, much less two. So—very different from your life."

"Yes, very."

"But even though it's crowded and noisy and all that, I like living in New York. There's so much to do. Cool restaurants, all kinds; you just put in your order and give them your credit card number and they bring the food to your door. And there are all these museums, and concerts, and Broadway shows, and the Hayden Planetarium, and ice-skating at Rockefeller Center, and the Central Park Zoo."

Max knows he's hogging the conversation, but there's so much he wants to tell her, he keeps going.

"There's one place I know you'd love," he says. "It's called the High Line. It used to be an elevated train. You've seen them in old movies, I'm sure, like train tracks up on stilts. So this one hadn't been used for years. It was all rickety and ugly, and they were going to tear it down. Then somebody got this great idea to turn it into a park. And it's just the most amazing thing! You have to climb up stairs to get to it, then it goes on and on for a mile and a half. You're way up high on this boardwalk with plants and trees and flowers and sculptures. Also sandwich places and ice cream stands and benches to sit on. You can look out at the Hudson River, or down at streets and parking lots, or up at the tall buildings. I guess that's what I like best about living in the city—all the really creative stuff you wouldn't find most places."

"I'd love to see it!"

"Well, you'll have to wait a while, like twenty, twenty-five years. In your 'now' it's still an elevated rail line. Maybe the trains are even running. Your turn."

"Hmm," she says, "let me think. Okay—how about music? Do you play an instrument?"

"I tried the clarinet," Max says, "but I didn't really like it."

"Well, I tried the piano and I loved it, but for some reason I had a hard time reading music. I don't know why. I can read words just fine. So I would just grind it out, slowly, painfully, practicing a piece over and over until I could play it from memory. Then the pieces started to get harder and I got more frustrated, so finally I quit."

"That's too bad."

"Wait," she says, "I'm not finished. I still loved music, so I started going through my dad's record collection. I'd just sit in the den with the lights off and listen with my eyes closed—blocking everything out, just listening. A lot of his stuff is modern, some of it really strange. Like this piece by George Crumb called 'Black Angels.' The first time I played it, it made me jump. It just sounded like noise, really intense, soft then loud, like the musicians were trying to murder their violins. But I turned down the volume and kept on listening. There wasn't a melody or anything. It was just, you know, this big wave of emotion. It was like I became a different person when I let that music inside of me. Or maybe I was inside the music. All I know is I wanted to be there. And when the music was over I wanted to go back. I do it a lot now, whenever I need to transform myself. It's my secret addiction. Does that sound crazy?"

She gives him this sort of wild-eyed look, making fun of her crazy self. She wants him to laugh, and he does.

"Not at all," Max says. "It sounds amazing. And by the way, here's a little tip from the future: tell your dad that when records go out of style and it's all about CDs—*pay no attention to the trend*! Save those records! Buy more! Because vinyl will come back big-time. People will start buying turntables again, and collecting records, because the sound is better. And he'll be so, so glad he didn't give his away."

"Thanks—though I'm trying to picture that conversation. 'Dad, this guy from the future told me to tell you . . .'"

"How about, 'Dad, I have this really strong female intuition that you should *not* give those records away'?"

"Much better. Your turn."

"Well," Max says. "What you said about listening to music? I felt something kind of like that when I was in my art class, working on this etching, scratching all these little lines onto a metal plate. I was slowly building up the darks and trying to get a gradation that the eye would read as shades of gray blending into black, so every stroke mattered; it had to be just right. Meanwhile, I had to mentally translate the scratch marks I was making on metal into the tiny black lines they'd create when the ink was rubbed in and it went through the press.

"So the part of my brain that makes plans and worries about stuff—it was busy thinking about the process. And that released this other part of me—kind of like what you said—that I didn't even know was there. I can't really describe it, but it was like I'd been running with a backpack full of bowling balls—then the backpack vanished, and I felt super light, like I could run forever. I could have stayed there all day, just scratching those lines. If I could actually have a job making art someday, it would be the greatest thing I could imagine."

"Maybe you will. Why not?"

"No reason, except it might mean starving in a garret... which is, I think, a really high place, like an attic, in a big old building. It's like living in a sixth-floor walk-up, so the rent is cheap. That's why artists go there to starve."

"Got it. But if your garret happens to be in Paris,

that might not be so—hold on, what is that? Over there. Light-colored. Big."

Max runs his eyes along the area ahead where the forest ends on open ground. Finally he sees it, the thing that doesn't belong.

"What is it?"

"I have no idea. Let's go see."

They come out of the forest onto a narrow path that runs along the bank of a stream. The stream is bigger and wilder than the creek beside Mozelle's cabin. The water rushes around large boulders, dances over rapids, creates little waterfalls. Definitely not something you'd want to wade in.

To their right, in the near distance, the path opens onto a clearing. And in the clearing there's a structure made of branches and twigs. It's a huge sort of upside-down basket in the shape of an igloo, with a small, arched door facing away from the stream and a round window on the side. The window strikes Max as kind of unnecessary, since you could see out perfectly well through the loose, basket-weave walls.

They walk around the structure, admiring its construction. It's wide enough for five or six to comfortably sit inside, and high enough in the middle that you could stand without bumping your head.

The structure is amazingly neat and well-built, considering that it's all made from natural materials, stuff found growing nearby or lying around in the forest. The window and doorway have been carefully finished with thin vines, woven around the edges in a braided pattern. Whoever built it wanted it to be beautiful.

"What do you think it's for?" Lila runs her fingers down the perfect curve of the wall.

"A clubhouse, maybe? But it won't keep the rain out, that's for sure."

"I bet it will when they finish it. This is just to hold it up, like the framing of a house. See over here, how they've woven in the vines, filling in the holes? Look how tightly it's packed together. I bet they plan to cover the whole thing like that. But wow, what a lot of work!"

Max wonders how a person would build such a thing, with the curving walls and high ceiling. The branches might be too stiff or too brittle to bend. And the ones that did bend might pop back straight the minute you let go of one end. So what would you do—tie them together with rope? And then how would you hold all the arched pieces together so they didn't collapse while you're trying to fasten them?

He runs a series of strategies through his mind. They all end in failure. To build something like this, he decides, you'd need a whole lot of helpers. And you'd have to be an artist *and* an engineer. Even then it would be crazy hard. No nails, no twine, no ladders.

"Look over here," Lila says. She points to the edge of the stream, where a bundle of vines has been set in the shallows, rocks holding them in place.

"Oh, I know what that's for," he says. "They're keeping the vines wet so they'll stay flexible." He's tempted to fish one out and try his hand at weaving. But that would be disrespectful. Like if Rosie decided to scratch a happy face onto his etching plate.

"Want to go in it? We came here to talk. Seems like the perfect place."

It does. Like it was put there just for them. So they crawl in and lie on their backs, side by side, looking up through the dome of branches at a perfect sky ringed by the swaying tops of trees. Max feels a deep ease spreading through him. It's like his bones are melting into the ground because there's nothing left that's tense or tight to hold his body together.

"Whose turn is it?" Lila says. Her voice sounds the way he feels—soft, peaceful, dreamy.

"I think it's yours, but I'd like to go again because I

have something really important to tell. It's my biggest thing, and no one knows about it except my family."

This is not exactly true. The police also know about it. But Max would rather not mention that part.

"All right."

"So, eight days ago my mother went off to help a friend. We know because she left a message on my dad's phone. Then she basically disappeared. We haven't heard from her since. We have no idea where she is, or who the mysterious friend is, or why he needs her help. Every day we hope to hear from her, and every day there's nothing. Sometimes I wonder if she's even still alive."

Lila is sitting up now, so Max sits up too. He wants to see her eyes, read her expression.

"Tell me everything, from the beginning," she says.

So he does. It takes ten minutes, maybe less, but he lays it all out. He even, on second thought, tells her about his dad's visit to the police station. And she listens, soaking it in, her mind working the whole time.

When she's sure he's finished, she leans in. "I'm guessing that isn't something your mom would normally do? Just going off like that. She's not an impulsive person?"

"No! Just the opposite. She's super responsible. Serious about stuff—I mean, she treats cancer patients. How could she *not* be?"

"So maybe she's super serious about this helping-a-friend thing. Maybe it's something really important."

"I would hope so, because she kind of left a mess behind."

"Because you're worried about her?"

"Well, yeah, of course we are. But it's way more than that. You know that thing people say about sharks, how they have to keep swimming or they sink?"

"This has to do with your mother?"

"Yes. Because Dad and Rosie and me—we're the sharks. And Mom's the one who keeps us swimming."

"What do you mean? Because she cooks the meals and makes you do your homework?"

"No, I literally mean she keeps us moving. Like on weekends, she'll say, 'Let's bake bread from scratch!' Or 'Why don't we take a picnic lunch to the park!' Or 'Let's go to the Japanese Garden in Brooklyn.' Or the zoo. Or the Egyptian section of the Met Museum. Or the High Line."

"Cool."

"Yeah, it is. Because none of us, on our own, would ever do those things. And after she left, we started to drift apart, each of us into our own little worlds. Not talking, mostly staring at screens, kind of blotting out the rest of the world—and each other. We're sinking, like the sharks.

Like we're not even a family anymore."

"Wow. You're right. That isn't good."

"And I just *miss* her, you know? Because when we're together, she's *all* there—not floating off somewhere else in her mind. She's listening to what I say, and thinking about it, and then she asks good questions because she wants to know more. It's like she really *sees* me. I can't explain it, but it's like this powerful booster shot of love that knocks out all the everyday bad stuff. And for that moment I feel like I'm the most important person in her world. Come to think of it—you're kind of like that too."

"Whoa, Max! Best! Compliment! Ever!"

"It explains the instant attraction."

Then she gets this sudden light-bulb-over-the-head expression. "Max?"

"What?"

"Can I ask you something? It'll sound unrelated, but it's not."

"Okay."

"Your grandparents have had their cabin for a long time, right?"

He nods.

"So your mom used to come here during the summers?"

"Yeah. Till she was a senior in high school."

She waits for him to catch up.

Finally he does.

"Omigod!" he says. He covers his mouth with his hands. "She could be here!"

"I know," she says. "And if you find her, you might also find—"

"The Mysterious Friend!"

"Want me to ask around? So you don't have to?"

"Please!"

"What's her name?"

"Dorothea. But everyone calls her Dory."

"All right," she says. "But, just so you know, if they usually came here in July instead of August, she'd already be gone."

"I don't know when they came, but I'll ask."

"Okay. Meanwhile, if she's here, I'll find her."

Chapter Nine

A LITTLE AFTER TEN THAT MORNING, the satellite phone rings. No one's expecting it, since Dad's the only one who has their number and they just talked to him a few hours ago. He'd be at the office now. So he wouldn't be calling unless there was news. Mozelle grabs the phone and they all run outside.

"Hello? Conrad?" They stand, breathless, watching Mozelle listen.

"Oh, that's wonderful," she finally says. "What a relief! Conrad, hold on a sec. Let me tell the kids." She holds the phone to her heart, grinning at Max and Rosie.

"He's heard from Dory! She's fine!"

They shriek and jump around till Mozelle makes them stop because she can't hear the rest of what he's saying. Which is apparently a lot because it takes quite a while. The few questions she asks strike Max as intentionally vague, the way grown-ups sometimes talk in code. It makes him wonder if there's more to this story than she's letting on. Like maybe the news isn't quite as cheery as she'd like them to believe. Then she hangs up without letting them talk to Dad.

"So, here's the story," she says. "This morning your dad got an email from a woman at a Starbucks in Maryland. She was there with her laptop, you know how people do, using a coffee shop as an office. So Dory went over to this woman and asked if she'd mind sending a message to her husband, since she'd lost her phone and couldn't call, and she really needed to check in."

Max gives her a look.

"I know, that wasn't true about the phone. But it was an easy way of explaining why she needed the woman to send the email for her. Okay?"

He'll go with that for now. He nods.

"She had the message already written down, with your dad's name and email address, so all she had to do was hand it over. The woman took it and sent the message.

When your dad got it, he emailed her back. But by then, Dory had gone."

That sounds really weird to Max, especially the part about writing everything out in advance. It's not what a person would normally do. He pictures his mother writing the message in a Starbucks restroom, one place she could be sure of privacy, where the Old Friend couldn't see what she was doing. Max pictures her folding it neatly, slipping it into her purse, then handing it to the laptop lady on the sly.

"What did Mom say?" Rosie asks, cutting to the chase.

"She said she was terribly sorry for being out of touch and making us worry. But she's fine. It's just that the 'project'—that's what she called it—is complicated and is taking longer than expected. She also said that it's truly important. She called it 'worthy.'"

"And that's it?"

"Your mom is fine, Max! She has an important job to do. When it's finished, she'll come home and tell us all about it. That's good news. All right?"

Max stays in the yard when they go back inside. He needs to think, to make some sense of his mother's weird behavior. The "worthy project." The secret handoff. No mention of who she's with or what they're doing in Maryland. It keeps building in his mind till he can't stand it any longer. So he goes back to the cabin and joins Mozelle in the kitchen, where she's cleaning out drawers.

"That's not the whole story, is it?" He says it quietly so Rosie won't hear.

"Not every detail, no."

"Details matter."

She looks at him straight on. "Yes," she says. "They do."

"Can I call Dad and talk to him myself?"

"You realize he's at work."

"And you think that's more important? Seriously?"

She recoils as if he'd slapped her. "No, I don't think that."

"Then what? You're protecting me? Because whatever it is you're hiding, lying won't change it. And we'll find out anyway, sooner or later."

"You know, Max—you might make it a life goal to be a little kinder. Dory is my child and I care about her every bit as much as you do."

"Sorry."

"If you want to call your father, then go ahead. But please be discreet about it."

She means Rosie, of course. For her, the crisis is over. Life is good. And, yeah—why mess with that?

Max hides the phone under his T-shirt so Rosie won't see it. Walks casually out the door, onto the porch. He stands there for a minute, as if enjoying the view, then goes down the steps and crosses the yard to the road. When he reaches a spot where he can no longer be seen from the cabin, he finds a rock to sit on, raises the antenna, and calls Dad.

He answers on the first ring. "Mozelle?"

"No, Dad, it's me." As he says this, he's struck by a memory. Standing in front of his parents' dresser, his mother's cell phone in his hand, the sharp realization that something was very wrong.

"Oh. Hi." Dad's tone is hard to read. Annoyed? Worried? Disappointed?

"I really need to talk to you. Mozelle said it was okay."

"Of course it's okay."

"Good. Because I have the feeling there's more about Mom than what Mozelle told us. Please, I want to know."

"Anything in particular? I mean, the good news is that she checked in and she's fine."

"So everyone keeps saying. But would you mind—"

"What, Max? No rush, but I *am* at work."

He lets that pass. "Would you please read me the email?"

He hears his father on the other end of the line drawing in a deep breath, then letting it out. Exasperation. Something like that.

"All right. I'll need to bring it up on my computer."

"I'll wait." He listens to the key clicks, the soft background hum of voices, doors closing, someone walking past his dad's office in high heels.

"All right. I have it now."

"And, Dad—can you read it word for word?"

"Oooo-kay. Word for word."

"All of it, all of the emails."

So he does.

Re: Message from Dory

From: Martha Calloway <mlcall1776@comcast.net>
To: conrad.sotelo1971@gmail.com

Dear Mr. Sotelo,
You don't know me, but I just met your wife, Dory, here at Starbucks. She asked me to forward a message to you because she's lost her phone and hasn't been able to get in touch. She wrote it all down so I'm just transcribing it here.

Dear Conrad—

I'm so, so sorry I've been out of touch for such a long time! I know you and the kids must be terribly worried. But

I'm absolutely fine. I just lost my phone. Meanwhile, the project has turned out to be much more complicated than I thought it would be—also far more important. Believe me when I say that it is truly worthy of my time and my expertise and even the inconvenience to you.

Please tell Mom I'm sorry to miss the cabin-cleaning trip. I'll make it up to all of you, I promise. If I don't get back to you again soon, don't worry. I'm just over-my-head busy. Okay?

Love to you, Max, Rosie, and Mom,

Dory

"What about the rest?"

"Hold your horses. Okay, so here's my email to her."

Re: Message from Dory

From: Conrad Sotelo <conrad.sotelo1971@gmail.com>
To: mlcall1776@comcast.net

Dear Ms. Calloway,
Thank you for forwarding my wife's message. Would you

mind letting her use your laptop very briefly so we can talk to each other directly? I would be extremely grateful.

Thanks,

Conrad Sotelo

"Now here's her reply."

"Dad? Wait. I didn't mean *literally* when I said word for word. You don't have to read the subject line and email addresses and stuff."

"That's a relief. Here goes."

Dear Mr. Sotelo,

I'm sorry, but she's already gone. She left right after she gave me the message.

Martha

Dear Martha (if I may),

That's very disappointing. Would you mind if I asked you a few quick questions? For starters, where exactly is this Starbucks? And was she alone when she left? She said she was going to help an old friend but didn't say who he was. Did you see him, and if so, can you describe him? And—I know this will sound silly, but can you describe my wife? Just so I'm sure it's her and not someone playing a prank on both of us. Anything else you can think of? As her message implied, we've been quite worried. So thank you for taking the time to send the message and to talk with me.

Gratefully,

Conrad

Dear Conrad,

Not a problem! I'll tell you what I can. I'm in Edgewater, MD. The woman who approached me was of average height, 40ish, with medium-length curly brown hair and wire-frame glasses. She was nicely dressed, slacks and a mustard-yellow jacket. She most definitely didn't look like a prankster, but she did seem nervous. When she approached me she stood at an angle, so she had to turn her head to talk. Most people would have pulled up a chair and chatted a bit first. But she just handed me the message and spoke (like I said, kind of sideways) a few words, basically that she'd lost her phone and needed to get a message to her husband, and would I mind sending it?

So I said okay, then looked down at the message to make sure the contact info and everything was there. And when I looked up, she was already on her way out. I'll be honest, it was strange. As I said, she seemed nervous the whole time. She kept glancing over at the pickup end of the counter, like she was worried someone there would see her talking to me. I assume that would be the man she left with. I didn't see his face, but he was pretty tall, slender, with dark hair. He was casually dressed in a blue shirt and jeans.

The message, by the way, was written on the back of a take-out menu from a local sandwich shop. Like she didn't have access to normal plain paper. That also seemed strange. She had it in her purse, ready to go. Just pulled it out and laid it on the table.

That's all I can remember. Sorry.
Martha

Did you see them leave? See their car?
Conrad

No, they just walked out the door. I didn't pay attention to the rest, just started sending the message.
M

P.S. Sorry, but that's all I know. Good luck!

So that was it, a polite kiss-off from Martha. Though to be fair, there was nothing more she could have done.

"Thanks," Max says.

"Look, I know this raises some questions. That's why I didn't want to share every detail with you in the first place. But let's focus on the positives. Your mom is alive and well. She's out in public, buying coffee, looking like her usual put-together self. She assured us that she's fine. If she were in danger and had the chance to send a secret message, she'd have asked Martha to call the police."

"But—"

"Let me finish. Yes, it's disturbing that she had to sneak around to send a message to her family. But I have the feeling her friend is worried about protecting himself, not trying to control her. And she made a big point about their 'project'—whatever it is—saying it was important and 'worthy.' There's no reason for her to say that if it isn't true. It's not like her friend was going to see the note. So I'm guessing it's legitimate, but in some way dangerous to him."

"Like what?"

"I don't know, Max. But I trust your mother's good judgment. I suggest you do the same. Can you try to do that?"

Max says yes, but it's a lie. "Trusting Mom's good judgment" feels like a cop-out. A dressed-up version of "Oh, well, she's probably fine." Like he's going with what he *wants* to believe, what's comfortable and easy, what makes *him* feel better. So he won't have to ask himself, *But what if she's not?*

After lunch they drive to Arnie's with four boxes of books. Max hauls them into the store and piles them up in front of "Arnie's Community Library"—which is a glorified name for a set of homemade bookshelves in a far corner of the store, over by the frozen foods.

His job done (and before anyone can suggest he also alphabetize and shelve the books), Max returns to the counter. Holds up his cell phone and charger for Arnie to see. Raises his eyebrows in a pleading look. Wordlessly, Arnie takes them, sets the phone on the counter by an electrical outlet, and plugs the charger in.

"You have Wi-Fi?"

"Yup. Everything's up-to-date in Millie's Crossing."

He sort of half sings it, doodley-doodley-doot, like it's lyrics to a song. Max suspects he's being mocked, but he's too grateful to care. He has an agenda, and evidence to gather, and he seriously wonders how people ever found answers to their questions before the internet was invented.

"The password is *millies123*."

It *would* be something like that, he thinks. But then Arnie probably doesn't have any data worth stealing. "Thanks," he says.

"Your grandma's trying to get your attention." Max turns to see Mozelle waving from the far end of the store.

He finds her with Rosie in the novelties section. It's mostly stuff for kids—puzzles, games, toys, crayons, comics—left over from the days when the compound was full of families. Arnie probably hasn't reordered in years—no market for that stuff anymore. So there are bare spots on the shelves, and a lot of the things look really old.

But among the offerings—apparently they weren't big sellers—is an impressive selection of blank journals. Three are the same brand that his mom used for her plant book. Max chooses one with a gray-blue cover and a black strip along the spine.

And, wonder of wonders, there's even a pencil sharpener. This is something he desperately needs. Because the colored pencils, after all those years in the toy box, duking it out with the Legos and blocks and the random remains of the Monopoly game, have all lost their points. And he does not relish the prospect of sharpening them with a kitchen knife. He imagines the blood. Worse, a sliced-off fingertip.

Rosie gets a book too, but hers is much bigger than his. It has a different kind of paper too, more of a drawing tablet than a journal. Also—a definite selling point for Rosie—there's a picture of a unicorn on the cover, a wreath of flowers around its neck.

Arnie comes over to chat, since they're the only customers in the store. Actually, they were the only ones there the last time too. Max wonders how he manages to stay in business.

"I guess things are about to change," Mozelle says as Rosie examines an especially ugly jigsaw puzzle.

"Oh yeah. A major renovation, starting next week. On the developer's dime, of course. Can't sell fancy houses without a fancy grocery store nearby."

"Seriously?" Mozelle said.

He makes a huffing sound. "You wouldn't *believe* how seriously! The man wants an espresso bar. Gonna set up a bakery out back, hire people to make breakfast rolls and pies and whatnot. And I've gotta have the right kind of mustard, and olive oils, and the balsam vinegars—a list as long as your arm. All this ready-made food, too—salads and sandwiches and stuff—so the fancy people don't have to cook for themselves."

"What about the library?"

"That was the deal breaker, the one thing I wasn't

going to budge on. So we're moving it to where my office is now. I want to put in some little chairs and tables so kids can sit there and read. If fancy kids like to read, that is."

"I assure you, as a former librarian, that fancy kids like to read the same as everybody else."

"Good to know."

Max takes his things up front, sets them on the counter, and checks his phone. It's up to 32 percent. Without unplugging it, he stands beside the counter, going through his messages. Finding nothing life-altering, he sends a text to Orson.

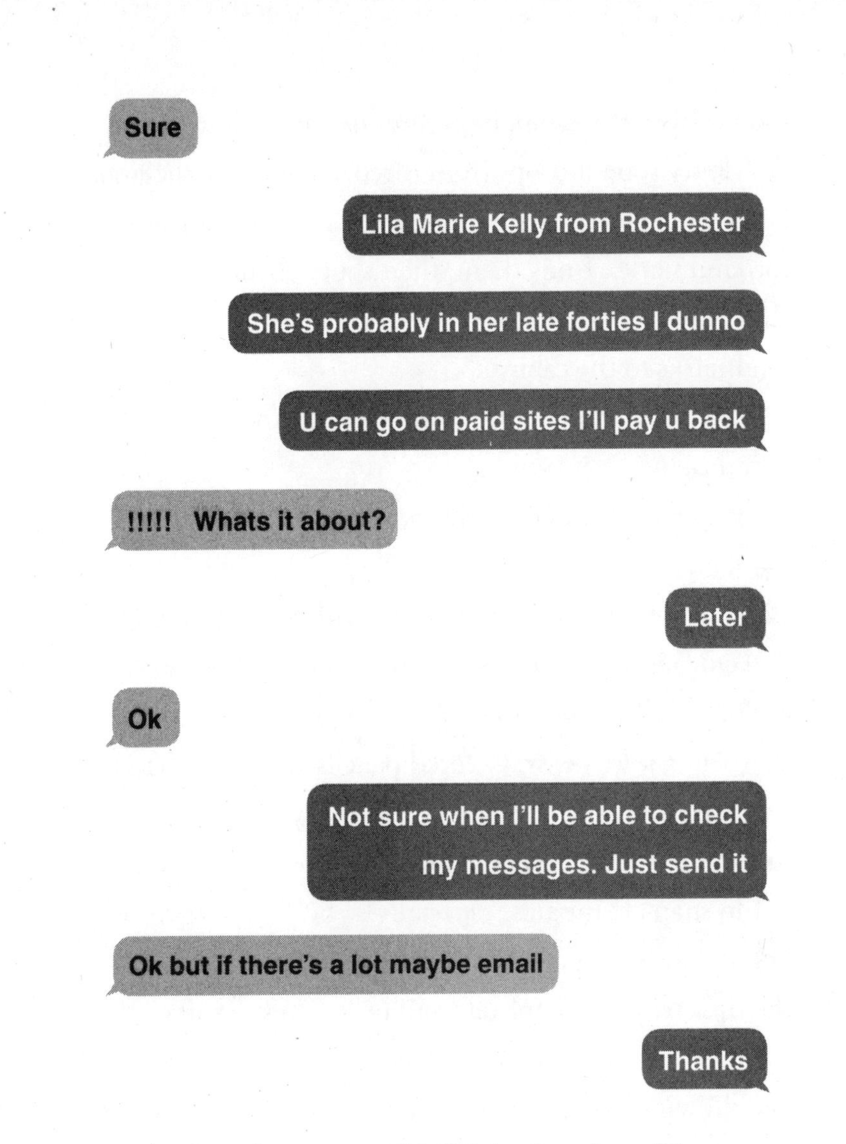

As they drive out of Millie's Crossing, Max stares silently at his phone. He feels sure that this will annoy Mozelle, but he has his reasons. He wants to determine the exact spot where the cellular coverage ends. If it's not too far from the cabin, he figures he can walk there.

Pretty soon it drops from three bars to two, then one. Seconds later, he gets NO SERVICE. He looks around for landmarks, finds them, then shuts off his phone and shifts his attention to the odometer. How far is it from his landmarks to the cabin?

Not very, it turns out. Maybe a mile and a half to the entrance.

He can definitely see this working.

Back at the cabin, Rosie settles in with her unicorn book and crayons. Max decides to sharpen his pencils outside so as not to make a mess in the house. But even with the new sharpener, it isn't easy. Colored pencils are softer than the regular kind. And he wants them really pointy so they'll make fine, delicate lines. This means being super careful not to snap off the tips, especially as he gets near the end of the sharpening process. Mostly he succeeds. Sometimes the tips snap off completely and he has to start all over.

By the time he returns to the cabin, Rosie is well into her drawing of the great Queen of Novo Yorkus. The queen is dressed like a Disney princess, a huge bejeweled crown on her head and a big poufy skirt. She has curly brown hair.

"I believe the queen wears glasses," Max says. "The

sort of invisible kind. So maybe use a pencil instead of that crayon? Draw it really light?"

"Okay," she says, skipping off in search of a pencil. Which is not that easy to find. Because people don't use them much anymore. Finally, after about ten minutes of looking, Mozelle discovers an ancient, stubby pencil in the back of a kitchen drawer. Then, of course, it has to be sharpened.

Meanwhile, Max opens his journal. He knows generally what he wants to do, but not what to call it, or how it might evolve by the time he's finished. So he leaves the title page blank.

He flips to the next page, where the dedication goes. He draws a large, neat square at the top of the page. Below it, he writes as neatly as he can:

for my mother
Dr. Dorothea Glickman-Sotelo
with love

The square is for his mother's portrait.

He starts by sketching it loosely with a light orange pencil, getting the proportions right, then framing the face, putting the features in. Gradually he works his way into it, moving from light to dark, adding details. When he draws the glasses, they are almost invisible, as they are in real life. Rosie leans over and stares.

"Ooooh, that's so good!" she says.

He actually thinks it *is* pretty good. So he decides to keep working on it, adding a polka-dot pattern to her blouse, icy-blue dots on a soft yellow-gold background. It's very neat, very delicate, right to the edge of the holding line. The added color makes the picture pop and balances the details of the face. Max stops drawing then and studies what he's done. It looks like her, definitely. He's pleased with the colors he chose, the balance of light and dark, the way it all fits in the frame. It fills him with pleasure.

He turns the page and waits, thinking. How does this story begin?

It begins, he decides, with the cabin.

So he slips the sharpener into his pocket, chooses several pencils in shades of brown and gray, and carries his journal outside. He sits on the ground some distance away and studies the scene—the building itself, but also the trees that embrace it on either side. That needs a lot of space, so he'll use both pages.

Resting the journal on his knees, he begins to draw.

By the time he returns, Rosie has moved on to the King of Novo Yorkus. His face is oval like an olive, leaning oddly. And there's something wonderful about it—the colors, the composition, the spontaneous lines, all the things Max's art teacher said were important. She obviously hasn't thought about any of that. It just came naturally. But to Max it looks like a work of modern art.

"That's awesome," he says.

"Really?"

"Absolutely. I'd frame it and put it on the wall. Maybe give it to Dad for Father's Day."

She lights up like one of their camp lamps, and Max feels an odd kind of pride. He has, without really planning to, made his sister happy. And that doesn't happen very often.

He goes back to his picture of the cabin, which he's sketched out in great detail. Now comes the fun part, shading the logs to make them look rounded, lighter on top where they're lit by the sun and darker where they fall into shadow. He draws stroke after careful stroke, creating an illusion of roundness but also the texture of rough wood. Then he goes in with more colors, like reds and yellows, purples and blues, mixing them softly with the brown of the logs and the green of the trees. He wants the colors to be richer, deeper, more interesting.

As he works, his mind floats. He thinks about Lila and her screechy music. About Rosie and her kingdom. Does Mozelle also have a place where she goes in her mind, like another room, a place where ideas flow like a river and fill her with peaceful joy? He hopes so. She deserves it.

By the time they have to clear the table for dinner, Max has finished the cabin. He's set the stage for what comes next—the real story. It's a perfect stopping place.

He puts his book and pencils away in the dresser drawer. Then he looks around the room that was once his mother's but is now starting to feel like his as well. His T-shirt-draped camping lantern. *Treasure Island* beside the unmade bed. His shoes in the middle of the floor.

The cabin is starting to feel that way too, like a place where he belongs. He has a routine going now. Three meals, two calls to Dad, bedtime reading, first sleep, stargazing, second sleep, dreams. The in-between, which had once stretched out like a vast Sahara of nothing-to-do, has been filled by a project that excites him. Rosie is behaving like the eight-year-old she is, which is definitely refreshing. There's even progress on the Mom front.

Lifted on a wave of contentment, Max sets the table without even being asked.

That night he goes to bed gladly, knowing Lila will be there when he wakes into his dream, for at least as many tomorrows as they still have. He lowers the blackout blind, reads about pirates till his eyes grow heavy, then lies in the darkness, feeling the silence that surrounds him.

He wonders if Mozelle might let them stay a few days longer, maybe even another week. Why not? Then, when Mom comes back, she could join them at the cabin. He feels sure she would want to see it one last time. And Dad could come too.

It'd be crowded, but they could manage. Mom and Dad could sleep in the big bed, Mozelle could take the single room, Rosie could have the couch, and Max would sleep on the floor. He wouldn't mind. He'd be thrilled, in fact, just to have them all here, together.

He tells himself this could happen. It *will* happen.

He'll ask Mozelle tomorrow.

Chapter Ten

THE GROUP IS BACK AT THE PICNIC TABLE—all but Zach, who's standing some distance away, a boomerang in his hand. He's about to send it flying over the field, which is currently empty. Max assumes it will then come flying back, since that's what boomerangs are supposed to do. And Zach will catch it like a pro.

"You two," Dee says. "Always late."

It took longer than Max expected to tell Lila his latest news—partly because it's complicated, but also because he had to keep stopping to explain things: that Starbucks is a chain of coffee shops, a laptop is a small personal computer you can carry around with you, a cell phone is a little wireless telephone that fits in your pocket, email is a way of sending messages electronically to other people's computers or phones, and Wi-Fi is how you get online without plugging in . . . and so on.

"Well, we're here now," Lila says, taking her seat on the bench and doing a little drumroll on the table. "And I have a game we can play if you want. When Zach is finished throwing his boomerang, that is."

"He's been at it for a while," Amber says. "Way past the point where it's entertaining."

"Hey, I heard that!"

"Come on. Put your toy away. It's not a group activity, and Lila has a game."

He flops down on the bench so hard they all feel it bounce. "What kind of game?"

"Well, something Max said yesterday got me thinking."

"Oh no! Not that!"

"Shut up, Zach," Amber says. "Lila? Yesterday you were thinking about . . . ?"

"Us, and the things we do together. I mean, they're fun, but sometimes they feel like we're just passing time. And we've known each other all these years, yet in lots of ways we don't know each other at all."

"There's a reason for that," Lenny says. "As you know."

"Yeah, but I wonder if it's a *good* reason. As long as we understand how things are—you know, back home, as compared to here—then what's the harm in going deeper? In sharing more about ourselves. Maybe even the different worlds we live in. Just this morning I learned about laptops, and cell phones, and Wi-Fi, and the internet, and text messages. I have seen the future!"

"Did you understand it?"

"Actually, Lenny? No."

This gets a laugh, and Max can tell she's won them over.

"So how does the game work?" Dee asks.

"Well, I came up with a list of questions and wrote each one down on a separate card. We'll take turns picking a question and answering it." She sets the cards in the middle of the table. "I'll go first, just to get us started, then we can go around the table, counterclockwise."

Max guesses she wants to go that way so that five others will have had their turns before they get around to Rosie. Give her a chance to see how it works.

Lila draws her card and reads it. "'Is it ever okay to tell a lie? And if so, when?'"

"Softball question!" Zach says.

She shrugs, because it really kind of is, but she goes

ahead with her answer anyway. "Yes to the first part. And an example would be telling a lie to keep from hurting somebody's feelings. So, if Dee asked if I liked her dress and I thought it was really ugly, I wouldn't say so. I'd say it looked great."

"That's kind of obvious," Lenny says. "But it wouldn't be such a softball question if you took it a little further."

"All right, how about this? You're in Germany during World War II and a Nazi comes up to you and says, 'Do you know if any of your neighbors are hiding Jews in their houses?' And you say, 'Of course not!' even though lots of them are."

"Obvious!"

"Wow, okay—what about lying because it's simpler? Because the answer to a question is complicated and boring and there's no reason to go into the whole thing."

"That's good, but I bet you can do better."

"Lenny, is this a class and you're my teacher?"

"No, Lila. I just think it's a really interesting question—which you wrote, so take a bow—but you need to keep at it. Let's say you're supposed to meet your friends at three. But you get busy doing stuff and forget the time and you end up keeping them waiting twenty minutes. Do you invent a terrible traffic jam?"

"Hmm. Well, I have actually done stuff like that. Is

it the right thing to do? I don't know. It would definitely get me off the hook, but I'd just be lying to save myself from looking like a jerk. Still, would it be better to tell the truth? Like, 'Hey, guys, I'm really sorry, but I was busy doing stuff and just forgot we were getting together'? Because that would hurt their feelings and our relationship."

"Getting better," Amber says. "We could keep this going all day."

"Let's not. Zach's turn."

Zach makes a big show of picking his card—putting a hand over his eyes and feeling around, sliding one out of the middle of the pile, then holding it up dramatically to read: "'What do you wish you were good at, but aren't?'"

Apparently, this is also a softball question, at least for Zach. He doesn't even have to think about it. "Singing," he says.

They all think this is hilarious. Because it's *so* not his image, with his buzz cut and jock walk and everything.

"No, seriously!" he says. "When I hear somebody who can really sing, it seems like the most powerful gift in the world. If I could sing like that, I'd want to do it all the time, just for the fun of it. Sadly, I was not blessed. I sound like a frog."

He gets another laugh with that, but Lenny is leaning

across the table, this semi-wicked expression on his face. "What kind of singing?" he asks. "Heavy metal?"

Zach slumps over, buries his face in his hands.

"What—*show tunes*?"

"Opera, okay? Like Pavarotti. We're Italian. It's a thing."

"But that's totally cool! See, Lila? You were right. Without your game we would never have known."

Zach looks at Lenny, not sure whether he is making fun of him or not.

"It was a compliment," Lenny says.

Max wonders how that conversation would have gone down if it had happened at his school. Whether Zach would forever be dubbed Pavarotti by the kind of guys who like to shove you up against lockers and say, "Oops, sorry!"

Still, he can feel this odd sort of tension, a bit of alpha-male testing of each other. Amber obviously senses it too, so she calls attention to herself by drawing a card and holding it aloft, then staring at it, wide-eyed, for a long time, like a soldier who's just been ordered to throw herself on a live grenade.

"Hmm," she finally says. "Can I pick another one?"

"If you're too scared to answer," Lila says.

"Ha, funny! Maybe that should be my answer."

"Oh! *That* one!"

"Yes, *that* one: 'What is your greatest fear?'"

They all agree that it's very ironic that Amber's afraid to answer the question about fear. Then they drop the jokes and wait, eager to hear how she'll answer it.

Which, as it happens, she never will because just then she's conveniently interrupted. A boy from the older group, the ones who dive-bombed their chess game with their soccer ball, comes running over. "Amber," he says, "we need you. Desperately."

"Why?"

"Oh, I don't know, because you're such a weak and wimpy player? No, wait, that's not it."

"My brother, Eric," she says to the group. Eric takes a bow.

"C'mon, *please*? You know you want to."

"Gosh, it's a tough call. I could sit here and answer a really hard, very personal question—or I could go out there and humiliate a bunch of eighth-grade wannabe jocks with my supreme womanly skills. Hard to decide."

It's not, really. She's already standing. She gives Lila a quick, apologetic look, then leaves with her brother, Zach trotting along behind.

"Their loss," Lenny says. "And besides, they've already answered. Zach wishes he could sing. Amber's afraid to answer personal questions. Now it's my turn."

"Go ahead," Lila says. "Dazzle us."

Like Zach, Lenny makes a production of picking his card. He stares suspiciously at the pile, as if a small, deadly snake might be lurking there. Creeps his hand in cautiously, then snatches his card away.

"It says: 'What is your greatest talent?'"

Dee groans. "Can he have five?"

"Down, girl," Lenny says. "Now, before I answer, just to be clear, a talent is not the same as an accomplishment. You haven't earned it so you can't take credit for it. You're just born with it. Right?"

"Agreed," Lila says.

"Then I'd have to say my greatest talent is my ability to remember things. I do *not* have, as I have said so often before, a photographic memory, because such a thing does not exist. But if I really focus on something I'm reading, or something I hear or see, I can remember it. And for some reason I'm especially good with numbers. I've worked hard to develop it—that's an accomplishment—but it was always there."

"You're so lucky," Max says. "I bet you make straight As without even trying."

Lenny waggles his hands as if conceding the truth of this statement. "But it's not all about remembering things.

Just spouting back stuff you got out of books is mindless. You're supposed to understand it, then analyze what you've learned and draw conclusions of your own. That's a whole other skill and it's a lot harder."

"I bet you can do that too."

"Okay, Dee," Lila says, moving the game along because things keep getting edgy with her questions, which was not her intention. "Your turn."

But Dee has been distracted by something in the distance. Max and Lila turn to see a boy carefully threading his way between the running and screaming kids on the playground and the soccer game on the field. He's frail and fair, his hair so blond it's almost white. His blue shirt is tucked into his pants and buttoned at the neck. All he needs is a tie to finish off the look, like he's on his way to a meeting of the junior chamber of commerce. He's carrying a white canvas bag and the bag looks heavy.

"Who's that?" Max asks.

"Just a kid I've noticed," Dee says. "New last year. He always comes late and he's always alone. I worry about him. He seems sad."

"His name is Henry," Lenny says. "And he's not sad. He's just different."

"You've talked to him?"

"Yeah, a little." He continues to watch as the boy

rounds the playground and moves closer to the forest's edge. "Sorry," he says. "Go ahead, Dee."

So she takes her card, sets it on the table, and stares at it for a while. "Hmm, this is a long one," she says, doing that nervous thing with her hair she seems to do a lot, running her fingers through it, pulling it back, then letting it fall forward again, half hiding her face. It's like she just got this brand-new hair for her birthday and she can't stop playing with it.

"So, okay, here it is. 'If you could do something really important and worthwhile but it would mean a big sacrifice for you and maybe for others too, would you still do it?' Want to give me a hint? Like what kind of really important thing are we talking about?"

Max knows. Lila's talking about his mom. Going off to help her friend while her family (the "others") get to sacrifice (without being consulted) their happiness and general well-being.

"Okay," Lila says. "What if someone you know is very sick—the details don't matter, this is just pretend. And he'll probably die if he doesn't have an operation, only he doesn't have the money to pay for it. And you just inherited some money with no limitations. You can spend it however you want. Would you give it to the sick person to pay for his operation?

"Or something smaller. Say you're on your way to a party with your friends when you find some little old lady's purse. All her important stuff is in it—her money and her driver's license and her glasses. So she's probably really upset that she lost it. Would you drop what you're doing, skip the party, and track the lady down? Call her and say the purse is safe so she won't be in a panic? Maybe even take it back to her?"

Dee nods. "Got it. So I'd have to say yes—within reason."

"You'd pay for the operation?" Max asks. "Instead of, say, saving it for college?"

"If I had the money, yes. My college plans versus a person's life or death—that's not really a hard choice."

"I'd like to think I'd be that generous," Lila says. "But you can't save everyone. The world is full of needy people."

"That's true," Lenny says. "But you can help the ones you know about, in this case, the neighbor. Or the little old lady."

"Would *you* do it?" Max asks. "Pay for the operation?"

"Yes. Though I'd probably look for a better solution first, like going around the neighborhood asking people to chip in. But if I was the only one who was willing, I wouldn't let the person die."

Max is glad Lila put in that question, though he wonders if she expected the answer she got. It reminds him of that old saying, that you can't really know a person till you've walked a mile in their shoes. And he realizes, with a minor shock, that what he's been feeling all along is not just fear and concern for his mom's safety—it's been anger. Now, for the first time, he's "walking in her shoes," seeing it from *her* point of view, and it's weirdly liberating.

He looks over at Lila. Whispers, "Thanks." And she seems to understand. A little flutter of her eyelashes, like a subtle form of Morse code, followed by a smile. "Okay, Rosie, you're next," she says. "But I'd like to look through the cards first if that's okay."

Nobody objects. They all want her to get an easy one.

"Okay, sweetie, take the one on top."

Rosie reads it haltingly. "'What have you done that you are proudest of?'"

"Maybe make it a little simpler?" Max suggests. "Just anything you're proud of?"

"No, that's okay," she says. "I know the answer. I was nice to Jacob in kindergarten when he dressed like a princess for Halloween. Everybody else made fun of him."

"Rosie! I never knew that!"

"Ms. Connor called Mom to tell her. She said I was the only one who played with him. And I should be really proud."

"Yes, you absolutely should," Dee says.

It's a solid gold moment. Rosie nuzzles into Dee, proud of herself all over again.

"Okay, last but not least. Max, finish the game."

"Which has been really great, by the way," he says. "A brilliant idea."

"Thanks. Though you might want to hold off on the compliments till you've actually read the question."

"Is that a warning?"

She shrugs, smiles like the Cheshire cat.

"All right, here it is, for the game! 'What is your biggest regret?'"

"Ouch!" Lenny says, doing that wicked-twinkly thing with his eyes that makes him look like Jeff Goldblum, only a whole lot younger.

As with Rosie's question, Max understands that adding "greatest" or "biggest" or "most" makes it much harder to answer. So he decides to come at it from a different direction—not what does he regret the most, but what does he do the *most often* that he always regrets? Then the answer is obvious.

"I regret that I haven't been nicer to my sister. Rosie, I

forget sometimes how little you are."

"That's okay," she says, her eyes like saucers, her voice almost a whisper.

"Not really. I will try to be nicer. I promise."

At this, she starts curling into herself, like a kitten or a baby, and emits a kitten-like whimper. It's the sort of thing that usually drives him crazy. But now that he's all walking-in-other-people's-shoes-aware, he understands that he's made her happy with his apology, only she doesn't know how to handle it. Also, she's embarrassed by all the attention.

So Max does their "Lookin' at you" thing, pointing two fingers at his eyes, then flipping his hand to point one at her. She giggles and does it back. Then the others pick it up, all of them Lookin' at Max, and Rosie laughs so hard she gets the hiccups.

When they're all done Lookin', Lila scoops up the cards, gives Max a quick, significant look, then swings her legs over the bench and gets up. This raises a certain level of curiosity, since Max is apparently staying put.

"I'm off to do a survey," she announces.

"Of a scientific nature?"

"Yes, Lenny, that is my intention."

"Need any help?"

"As it happens, I don't."

"Ohhhhkay."

Then she's off, starting at the playground, talking to the little kids one by one, then moving on to the ball team. This proves to be more of an undertaking, since they're not inclined to accommodate Lila by pausing their game to answer questions. So she has to grab them on the fly. Anyone not in motion is fair game.

Max watches her intently as she goes from person to person asking her simple yes-or-no question: Do you know a girl named Dory?

He'd asked Mozelle which month they usually came to the cabin and she said August. Which means that, unless his mom has already aged out—which is certainly possible—she has to be here. She could be any one of the squealing tots on the playground. Or a teen baking on the pier. Or a girl kicking a ball around on the playing field. And though the prospect of meeting his mother's younger self is definitely unnerving, it might help him find his grown-up mom in the real world. So, definitely worth the discomfort.

He wonders how Lila can possibly keep all the players straight when they're constantly in motion. How can she remember who she's asked and who she hasn't? Then again, it might not matter. They're a group of friends, after all. They know one another's names.

Asking just a few should be enough.

But Lila is being thorough, dogged, and determined, and Max is attuned to her every move. Which is why, when one of the girls leaves the game and goes to stand on the sidelines, he notices. There's something odd about the way she moves, slowly, like she's totally exhausted. And her odd stillness as she stands there, staring into the distance.

Amber runs past her and waves but the limp girl doesn't respond. It's as if she's frozen in place. Then slowly she begins to fade, becomes transparent, and disappears.

He gasps.

"Don't worry," Dee says. "It's normal. She just woke up, that's all."

"That's *so* creepy!"

"You get used to it."

Till this moment he hasn't considered the logistics of waking. Personally, all he remembers is gradually sliding into a deep fog, then emerging again to find himself in the cabin, heavy with sleep and safe in his bed.

"What's with the scientific survey?" Lenny asks. "She seems very determined."

"No clue," Max lies, crossing his fingers under the table.

She's left the playing field now and has moved on to

the teens stretched out on the pier. Which—he's sure this is not his imagination—are not as many as there had been just a few minutes ago. There are even empty spots where some of them had been. They must have woken too. Even their towels are gone.

The survey complete, Lila heads back to the picnic table, her shoulders slumped, her head down. When she's about six yards away, she looks up at Max and he sees it on her face.

The answer is no. His mother isn't there.

Chapter Eleven

HE WAKES TO RAIN, the kind with fat, heavy drops that fall straight down. In the living room, it's just Mozelle, reading and drinking her coffee. Rosie's still asleep because it's a sleep-in kind of morning. Gray and quiet, the soothing patter of rain on the roof.

Mozelle points toward the kitchen, where something sweet is warming in the oven. But Max joins her at the table instead. He wants to talk before Rosie gets up.

"I've been thinking about Mom and the 'worthy' project."

"Oh?" She marks her place and closes the book. Gives him her full attention.

"Yeah. It's like a puzzle. We have these pieces of a story that somehow fit together. And when they do, it'll all make sense. I mean, there aren't even that many pieces. It shouldn't be too hard."

"So what are the pieces?"

"Well, the friend told Mom he needed her to help because she's a doctor. So, that's one. And whatever his project is, it's complicated or hard in some way. A lot of work involved. Third, it's somehow dangerous to the friend, which is why he's being so secretive. And four, Mom said the project is important and worthy. So: medical, complicated, dangerous, and worthy. Just four pieces. How many scenarios could fit that description?"

Mozelle stares into the middle distance and blinks, like this is a new approach and she's running it through her mind. "Good reasoning, Max."

"And?"

"Well, the dangerous-but-worthy conflict feels like the key. That really narrows it down. So we have to ask, what's the source of the danger? It wouldn't be the police—unless, of course, they were so-called bad cops and he's exposing them." Then she sucks in breath so hard it makes her cough. "That's it!"

"Bad cops?"

"No. Police corruption isn't related to medicine. But it could be some other kind of wrongdoing that the friend has discovered and wants to expose." Suddenly, her hands go up, like she's telling Max to *stop*, when in fact he isn't doing anything.

"What?"

"Medicine! A hospital that's overcharging patients or shielding incompetent doctors. A lab that's doing sloppy research that could have major public health consequences, mishandling smallpox samples, something like that. Or a pharmaceutical company that's been promoting drugs they know are harmful or useless. I'll bet the friend is a whistleblower!"

"A what?"

"You know how in sports, referees blow a whistle to stop the game when there's been a foul? This is calling attention to a different kind of foul, which is why they call it that. Like in the famous tobacco case. The Philip Morris Company knew their cigarettes were highly addictive and that smoking caused cancer. They even had internal studies to prove it. But they were making so much money, they hid the evidence and went on selling cigarettes. They even added chemicals to make them more addictive."

"Whoa, nasty!"

"Yes. A classic case of heartless greed. Fortunately, someone on the inside exposed what the company was doing, 'blew the whistle' on big tobacco. It was a brave thing to do and there were consequences for him. He lost his job and the security people harassed him, but he saved a lot of lives. That fits, don't you think? Dangerous to the friend but important and worthy?"

"Absolutely!"

"It would explain why they're hiding out in Maryland, why he's being so cautious. It even explains why it's taking so long—they're probably going through mountains of technical data to make sure their case is solid before they go public."

"We need to call Dad."

"Yes. It won't help us find her, but whenever she connects again, he'll have done his homework and can give them some solid legal advice."

"Why would they need that? They're the good guys."

"A person can get in big trouble for taking documents like that. Maybe even for helping someone who has. There are laws to protect whistleblowers, but it's important to know what they are so you don't cross a line. It's not your dad's field of practice, but he'll know who to ask."

"What—like Mom could go to jail? Is that what you're saying?"

"I don't think so, Max. But I really wish she'd call. And when she does, your dad needs to be ready to advise her. That's all I meant."

She gets the phone off the coffee table and opens the door. A wave of cool, wet air floats in. Going out into the yard is not an option. If anything, the rain is heavier now. So they stand at the edge of the porch to call, the phone's antenna angled toward some invisible satellite, out there in space, circling the earth, far beyond the clouds.

"Conrad," Mozelle says, "Max and I have come up with a pretty good guess about what Dory and her friend are doing. I think you'll like it. I'm also pretty sure they'll need a lawyer."

Max returns to his book—his spirits lifted, his anger gone, the backpack full of bowling balls laid down for now.

The journal opens naturally to his picture of the cabin. Now he turns the page, runs his finger down the gutter to flatten it a little, and considers what to do next. Maybe introduce the cast of characters, with a one-page portrait of each? After that, it'll be scenes with action and backgrounds and dialogue in word balloons. Which he's really eager to get to.

So he thinks, *What if I begin with the first time I met Lila?* It would be a scene instead of a portrait, but it would also introduce the first two characters. Then he could do the others later. Because really, his book is about the two of them. Their friends are just a subplot.

Since the picture will show them talking to each other, they'll have to be seen from the side, which is going to be harder. He's good at drawing faces from the front, kind of has a system for it, but profiles not so much. Then again, if he wants to be an artist, it's something he'll need to learn.

So: Max will be on the left and Lila on the right, with trees in the background. In a moment of inspiration, he decides to put a big tree smack dab in the middle, between the two pages, about a quarter inch of trunk on either side. Since the trunk is vertical, nothing looks distorted. And it can be thicker or thinner, depending on how firmly you open the book.

Genius!

As before, he sketches very lightly in pale orange to establish the figures, their size and position. Then, gradually working his way into it, he does his best to make them stand in a natural way, worries about how to arrange their arms and hands.

This is the hardest part for him, the initial drawing. But gradually it comes together, till he's ready to start moving into the darker colors.

Still, the ghost of his orange under-drawing is bound to show—though maybe, on second thought, that's not a problem. Because he actually kind of likes the way it looks. He decides to make the pale orange halo a hallmark of his personal style.

So there they are: Max standing tall, gazing down, looking kind of dorky. Lila, tiny and ramrod straight, gazes up at him, her arms folded confidently across her chest. Her bright hair flowing down her back.

Over Max's head is a word balloon that says, "I like your posture! It makes you look bold!" Her word balloon, surrounded by question marks, says, "Whaaaat???" It's pretty funny. It even sort of looks like Lila.

The rain finally stops. Half an hour later, the sky is completely clear. By then Max is stiff from hunching over the table and his brain is numb from thinking so hard. He needs to move around. So he goes to his room, gets his phone from the drawer, and hides it in his pocket.

"I think I'll take a walk," he tells Mozelle. "I may be gone awhile." He hears himself say that and winces. He sounds just like Mom.

"Are you going to the lake?" Rosie asks hopefully.

"No. Up the road toward Arnie's."

"Why not just walk around the compound," Mozelle

says, "where there isn't any traffic?"

He sighs. Unwilling to tell an outright lie, he might as well tell the truth. "Okay," he says, "here's the story. On our way back from Arnie's I watched to see where the cell phone signal ended. I know where that is. Just a little over a mile."

"We have a satellite phone, Max. You can make calls from here."

"This is texting and stuff. Downloading documents. You need a smartphone for that. It's something I need to research."

He mentally writes Mozelle's thought balloon:

Except the "blankety-blank" part was his addition. Mozelle is way too dignified to think like that.

"It's important to me," he says. "I'll spend like two minutes on the phone, downloading the material, that's all. Then I'll come back."

She nods, though he can tell she doesn't like it. "You know to walk against the traffic, right?"

He can't resist. "What traffic?"

"Whatever traffic there might be. Stay on the left-hand side so you can see the cars approaching. You don't want them coming up behind you."

"All right."

"Can I come?" Rosie says.

"No!" They both say it at the same time.

There's a single text from Orson: "check your email." So he does.

And, yeah, there's definitely a lot of material, all of it packed into one long cut-and-pasted paragraph that's going to be a terrible slog to get through. Spaces or indents would have helped, but this is Orson, and that's not the kind of thing he thinks about.

Max sends him a quick text: "Thanks. More later." Then he sits on the side of the road to read about Lila's life.

On the one hand, this is solid gold evidence—that Lila truly exists, that the weird time disparity thing is real, and that Max, without a doubt, is not delusional.

On the other hand, it's going to be painful. It's one thing to accept the general idea that they're divided by a Great River of Time. It's something else altogether to see it on her Facebook page. But it's not like he can close the email and leave it sitting there like a ticking bomb. And since his battery life is still pretty low, even after topping it up at Arnie's, he'd better read it while he can.

So. Lila is forty-eight years old.

She's married to a man named Robert Barnstone.

They live in Boston with their two sons, William and Ethan. The address means nothing to Max since he's never been to Boston and doesn't know the neighborhoods. He assumes it's someplace nice.

She graduated from Cornell, then got a law degree from the University of Pennsylvania. Now she works as a public defender. He's not sure what that is. Some special kind of lawyer. He'll google it when he finishes Orson's email.

He pictures the grown-up Lila standing in a courtroom talking to a jury. He can totally see it, that fierce look she gets when she feels strongly about something. Her boldness. Her posture.

Scrolling down, there's more. Lila helped start a nonprofit organization that brings authors into prisons to teach creative writing to the inmates. She probably does some of the teaching herself since, in addition to being a lawyer, she's also an author. She's written a book of poetry called *Dreams Before Dawn*, which Max is *so* going to buy when he gets home!

Best of all, after scrolling through the dense and endless column of type, there's a picture. It looks like it was taken at some big event, probably one of those fundraiser things, because she's all dressed up and standing with her husband, posing for a photographer. She looks different, but then, of course she would. She's older, for one thing, her face is fuller, and she wears her hair short now—less shampoo commercial and more professional woman. But she's still tiny, the top of her head just reaching her husband's clavicle, and she still stands in a way that dares you to cross her.

He googles *public defender* and learns that, basically, it's a lawyer who is paid by the government to represent poor clients, so that all defendants, no matter who they are, can be equal before the law. So yeah, that fits. A very Lila sort of thing to do.

He shuts down his phone and sits there for a while. He can't decide whether he's happy that things turned out so well for her, with a nice family and an important job and real purpose in her life. Or sad because now he knows deep down for sure that the friendship they have is absolutely, without a doubt, temporary.

But at least he'll have his book—a record of their time

together, the things they said and did. So he can open it any time he wants and relive this incredibly mind-blowing week in his life.

It makes him want to work harder, to make sure his book is worthy of the subject. He won't leave anything out. Which means he'll probably—definitely!—still be working on it months after school has started.

He now thinks maybe it won't just be pictures and word balloons. Because some things need more words, whole paragraphs, maybe a full page, like those things Lila told him, about her ancestors and her dad's music, and the things he told her, not to mention the things they have yet to share. That's way too much to fit in a balloon. And besides, the pictures would detract from the words themselves. So he'll mix in pages of text with pages with art.

As he walks back to the compound—having dutifully crossed the road so he is once again on the left, facing the nonexistent traffic—he thinks about books and permanence.

Mark Twain, for example. He wrote *Huckleberry Finn* a long, long time ago. He's dead now—probably his children and grandchildren and great-grandchildren are too—but his words and ideas are still as fresh and alive as they were when he sat at his old-fashioned desk and wrote them with (just guessing here) a quill pen. It's kind of like their dream world—all of them having conversations with each other across the space of time. Which, when you think about it, is pretty amazing.

By the time Max gets back to the cabin, Mozelle and Rosie are eating lunch. He assures Mozelle that he managed to survive the dangers of an empty rural road, then goes to the kitchen to make a cheese sandwich.

"The world still functioning out there?" Mozelle calls from the living room.

"Yup. Still spinning in space."

Max makes up four more boxes for Mozelle, pulling open the flat cardboard, folding down the bottom flaps, and securing them with strapping tape. He even folds down the top flaps to make it easier for her to fill the boxes.

He's suddenly aware that, from the moment they arrived at the cabin, all she's done is work. Shopping, cooking, packing. Finding Rosie things to do. Putting up with Max and his moods.

"What if Rosie and I cook dinner tonight?" he says.

She looks up from a pile of papers she's been going through. "Well, that would be really dandy," she says.

"Just, you know, show me where things are and stuff? We'll do the rest."

"It's a plan." She's fighting back a grin, but he doesn't

mind. She's just pleased and surprised, and that's what he intended.

On a roll now, feeling virtuous, he joins Rosie at the table and helps her with her map. He lets her use one of his light-colored pencils to sketch it all out first. "Then you can go over it with your crayons later." She seems to grasp the wisdom in this approach.

They draw roads and mountains, villages and farms, and a tiny castle surrounded by walls. For excitement, Max introduces a Swamp of Despair, a Crocodile River, and a Volcano of Doom. Then Rosie says she wants some nice things too, so they add a Spring of Eternal Life and the Flower Field of Joy.

The map is pretty crowded with all those magical places. And no matter how Max tries to guide her, she draws everything too big. So there's not much space between one thing and another. That would bother Max a lot, but Max is not Rosie, and Rosie seems to think it's right up there with the *Mona Lisa*. So they call it done, turn the page, and prepare to draw the Castle of Novo Yorkus.

When the castle is sketched out, Max leaves her to finish it and goes back to his own book, thinking ahead now, planning it out in his mind. After the cast of characters is done, he'll do the chess scene, which he knows will be super hard, with seven people, some seen from the back, some from the side, all that. Plus perspective for the table and the chessboard, and also the lake in the background. But he thinks he can handle it. He'll just have to work out every detail in advance with his magic orange pencil.

But that'll just be setting the scene, after which he'll continue the action in a series of smaller close-ups, several panels to a page, comics style:

The ball flying in.

The ball smashing into the chess game, pieces scattering every which way.

Rosie screaming.

People crawling on the ground to gather up the pieces.

Lenny looking triumphant as he puts the pieces back where they belong.

And definitely one of Rosie taking her victory lap—just before Max drags her off to the cabin to tell Mozelle they're okay.

Wow, he could keep that one scene going for five or six spreads.

It's going to be a long book. He may need a volume two. Maybe Mozelle will buy him a second journal at Arnie's so they'll match.

But, before all that—slow down, Max!—he needs to do the portraits of his cast of characters. He's already introduced Lila in the "meet cute" scene. But she deserves a proper face-front portrait, same as the others. And if he leaves himself out but includes Rosie, it fits perfectly into three spreads.

So that's where he starts, Lila in her blue-and-white dress.

He puts his whole heart into it, determined to give her real expression, not just a generic pretty face. Her small mouth, large eyes, kind of wide-set. Straight eyebrows. And the freckles, that's the hardest part—like, how to make them look like fairy dust and not a case of the measles?

Soft, soft, soft, that's the answer. Just a touch of the pencil tip, then a slight smudging motion with his finger. And being super careful where they go. Not too many, mostly across her nose and cheeks.

Then a punch of blue in her eyes, a bit more orange in the hair. When he comes to the end, it's like he's been holding his breath for hours. He's amazed by what he's done.

It looks, truly looks, like Lila.

When the light starts to fade, Max puts his things away and goes into the kitchen with Mozelle. They decide on pasta with a simple salad.

Mozelle is usually an old-fashioned cook who makes everything from scratch. But that's not practical for such a short stay, when there's hardly anything in the pantry. And it'd be wasteful to buy a ton of stuff, then throw half of it away.

Also, she's been kinda busy.

So, sauce out of a jar it is—Newman's Own Sockarooni Sauce (Peppers, Spices, & the Whole Shebang!)—which she chose because all the profits go to charity. Also the jar features a picture of a movie star from back in the day. Mozelle says he's dreamy, though sadly no longer with us.

She asks Max if he'd like to make garlic bread and he says sure. So she talks him through it all, which takes about seven minutes, then brews herself a cup of tea and goes to put her feet up in the living room. Which, he realizes, is way overdue.

Rosie appears. He gives her the task of slicing the Italian bread, being careful with the knife and cutting only partway through, so the loaf stays connected at the bottom. And when she's done that, she will slip a tiny pat of butter between each slice. He cuts a garlic clove into slivers so she can tuck them in along with the butter. Then it'll all go into the oven and bake up crispy and nice.

Max organizes the rest of his tasks the same way he

plans out his pictures, except he's calculating time instead of space on a page. Setting water on to boil for the spaghetti, adding the right amount of salt. Then heating up the sauce at a simmer. Washing the lettuce, drying it in a dish towel. Adding some Parmesan cheese, slicing green onions. (Newman's Own Italian Dressing will be added at the very last minute so the salad won't get soggy.)

"This is fun," Rosie says, making slow work of the garlic bread, which is not a problem at all. The oven is warming. It'll be ready whenever Rosie is.

He drops the spaghetti into the pot and boiling water erupts as if in protest. He and Rosie jump back in alarm, then laugh as it settles, making a bit of a mess on the stovetop, but oh well. And at that moment, if only for a little while, Max is content—with this day, with himself—and cautiously hopeful about his mom.

Chapter Twelve

THE GROUP HAS GATHERED DOWN by the lake. They're perched on the smaller boulders, waiting for the last few to arrive. Rosie's wearing her favorite pink T-shirt with the sequined panda on the front and her pull-on pink tutu skirt. To this outfit she added a wide-brimmed sun hat and little red sunglasses, raising the cuteness factor to the level of a viral meme.

"Hi," Max says. "It's me, Rosie's brother."

"I don't know how you stand it," Dee says, "living in her shadow as you do."

"It's the burden I bear."

Lenny has already stripped to his swim trunks and is wading timidly into the water, tossing a lurid green tennis ball from hand to hand like a juggler. "C'mon," he calls. "Let's get moving."

"Oh, get moving yourself," Zach says cheerfully. "I'm waiting for Amber."

Swimming, Max thinks, suddenly realizing that, without knowing or planning it, he's wearing a swimsuit under his cargo shorts. He has even brought a towel. If only real life were like that—the cosmos preparing you for whatever lies ahead with no effort required on your part.

"She can find us, Zach. We're not invisible."

So they follow Lenny's lead and get ready for their swim. Rosie removes her T-shirt and skirt and lays them reverently on a rock. Her super-cute smiling-shark swimsuit now revealed, she dolls herself up again.

"Don't wear those in the water," Max says. "You'll lose your glasses and ruin the hat."

"Oh," she says, reluctantly taking them off, laying them carefully beside the rest of her outfit.

Then Amber arrives, in her suit and ready to go.

"Finally!" Lenny says.

"I like to make an entrance."

She has the look of a swimmer, with distinct muscles

in her shoulders and arms. She's probably on some competitive team wherever it is she lives. As if to prove it, she makes a beautiful shallow dive into the water.

Lenny's up to his waist now, taking it one careful step at a time. Or at least that was his original plan before Amber started splashing him. Now Lenny is screaming.

"Just how cold is it?" Max asks Dee.

She doesn't answer, just smiles.

They call the game a "story circle" and it features Lenny's tennis ball. When Max asks Lila how it's played, she just says it's easy, he'll see. But it's alphabetical.

Lenny begins by tossing the ball to Dee. Which apparently means she goes first.

"I gave an APPLE to the teacher," she says.

"Boo!" Zach calls. "That's totally beneath you."

"Well, okay then—I checked the ASTRONOMICAL tables." Then she pitches the ball to Zach.

"And I saw that there would be a BRIGHT full moon that night." The ball goes to Amber next.

"So I'd be able to see the moon's CRATERS with my telescope."

Max is not prepared when the ball comes to him.

"Um," he says, thinking fast. "I set up the telescope as soon as it got DARK." He passes the ball to Lila.

"By the time I'd finished EATING dinner, the moon had started to rise." Lila looks at Rosie, who is right beside Dee, so presumably Dee will help her. Rosie holds out her hands and Lila gently tosses the ball, which Rosie misses but quickly retrieves. Dee leans down and whispers something. Rosie whispers back.

All eyes are on her as she takes a big breath and proudly delivers her line. "Looking at the moon was FUN!"

"Perfect ending!" Lila says.

Three more story circles follow. The last one, ARTISTS, goes all the way through the alphabet, including X-RAY technology for revealing underpainting, and finishing with ZERO chance that Rembrandt will ever be forgotten.

That's way too long for Max. The water is shockingly cold, and he hasn't really adjusted. Or rather, he did adjust, sort of, for a while, then at some point the warmth started draining from his body, so that now he's wondering if this is how it feels to be a corpse. Not good, that's for sure.

So when the story circle breaks up and they move on to Marco Polo, he uses Rosie—who is shivering and wearing her anxious face—as an excuse to get out of the water. Lila joins them. Dee follows soon after.

Max wonders if the icy swim is some kind of twisted tradition, like those polar-bear plunges people famously do on New Year's mornings. It's definitely not his idea of fun. On the other hand, it'll make an awesome picture in his book—multiple close-ups of Max as he gradually turns deeper and deeper shades of blue.

They towel off and get dressed, then warm themselves in the sun while Amber swims laps using a variety of powerful strokes and Lenny plays ball with Zach. Maybe they simply lack nerve endings, Max thinks. Or grew up in Siberia.

Dee is leaning forward, methodically squeezing water from her hair, strand by strand, working from the scalp all the way down to the ends. There's something odd and fascinating about this careful effort of hers, rather like milking a cow.

"Max," Lila says in his quiet voice. "Want to head off on our own for a while?"

"Sure," he says, sliding off the rock. "We could go back to the structure."

"Yeah, perfect. But let's take the path this time. I don't want to walk through the woods in sandals."

Max hasn't considered this. Or that fact that he's also wearing sandals. Sandals—and this is interesting—that *he doesn't actually own*. His cosmic dresser, who made sure he had a swimsuit and towel, has taken care of his footwear too.

Yet another angle of the dream world. Wonderful and strange.

The path has a different feel from walking through the forest, which was full of atmosphere and an exciting hint of something sinister lurking nearby. Watching them pass. Maybe it's friendly, maybe it's not.

But the trail is open and bright and almost too beautiful to be real. They walk on a cushion of fallen leaves, the sunlight broken by the shimmering shadows of the trees off to their right. And beside them on the left the rushing stream, foaming over rocks, clear as glass along the edges where the water is still.

It's possibly the most restful place he's ever been. More than that, it feels like a sacred space, to be treated with reverence. So they walk softly without speaking.

Max tries to capture every little detail, knowing he can never do it justice in a drawing, but still determined to try. He studies the shapes of the trees, the patterns of light and dark. Notes the almost silver sheen of the leaves beneath his feet.

He concentrates all his senses now—the sound of running water, the soft tread of Lila's steps, walking ahead of him. There's a smell of water too—who would have thought it? Mossy, damp, mineral-fresh. And the trees, of course, and the smell of the sun bringing everything to life.

He's so lost in the moment, he almost runs into Lila when she stops. He steps back, then to the side to see what's ahead.

It's the new boy, Henry, standing in a shaft of sunlight, a fistful of trimmed vines in one hand, a cutting tool in the other. His face and pale hair, caught by the sun, glow cool and almost white.

"Hi," Lila says.

Henry says hi, but he doesn't move.

"I'm Lila. I've seen you around, but we've never met. You're Henry, right?"

He nods.

"And this is my friend Max."

It's like she's taming a frightened fawn—the gentle, coaxing tone of her voice, as if she's afraid any sudden move will send him bounding away into the forest. "We were just walking, you know . . . yesterday . . . and we came upon this really amazing structure. I mean, wow!"

Silence.

"Did you build it?"

He nods.

"By *yourself*?"

He nods again.

Max steps a little closer, slowly, respectfully. "Henry," he says, "I want to say that I'm totally amazed you could do that. And I wonder, would you mind telling me your whole name? I want to know it because someday, in the real world, I have the feeling you're going to be famous."

There's a moment of silence. Then: "Henry Aaron Rutledge."

"It's an honor to meet you, Henry Rutledge. You are a true artist. That's what I want to be when I grow up—but you already are."

"Thank you," he says.

Henry hasn't moved a muscle this whole time except to nod. He's waiting for them to vacate his space so he can get on with his work.

"I think we'd better leave now," Lila says.

Max touches her shoulder. *Wait.*

"But we'd like to come back sometime," he says. "If that's okay. To see what you're doing."

Henry nods, yes.

And then, to Max's astonishment: "You can help if you want."

Chapter Thirteen

MAX HAD PLANNED TO FINISH his cast of characters that morning. The original plan was for there to be six, which will fit perfectly in three spreads, a separate page for each. But now he's rethinking it. Because he wants to include Henry too, and that makes seven, leaving the facing page empty.

Or—a new thought!—it could be a full double page: Henry surrounded by all that beautiful scenery, as if the path and the forest and the rushing water were characters in the story too. This feels deeply appropriate.

So he skips ahead, leaving the right number of blank

pages for the rest of the group. He'll get back to them later, but he wants to draw Henry now, while the scene is fresh in his mind.

He makes the figure small, standing some distance away from the viewer. The stream is to his left, trees are to his right, and the path disappears into background. Angling down from the upper right, a bold shaft of sunlight pours over Henry's face, causing it to glow like a full summer moon, lighting up his pale hair like the halo of a saint. The rest of him is in soft shadow.

Max is thrilled with the effect. And pleased with Henry's wide-eyed expression—not fear exactly, more like extreme caution. The narrow shoulders, the skinny arms hanging down, his hands clutching the vines and the cutting tool.

He works on it for hours, deepening the darks in the trees, trying to get the transparency of the water. It's the most difficult picture he's ever attempted, and he watches in wonder as it grows deeper and more complex—until suddenly he knows, with some blessed wisdom he hasn't yet earned, that it's time to stop. Any more and it'll be overworked and will lose the perfect balance of light and color.

There's only one thing left to do. He takes a black

pencil, sharpens it, and finds a spot on the lower left where the path is a soft silver gray. There he writes, as neatly as he can,

Henry Aaron Rutledge

He stops and studies what he's done. It's better than anything he'd ever even imagined he could do. He's so pumped, he finds himself chasing that feeling, wanting to do more pictures with mood and setting and atmosphere. Finally he gets up and walks in circles on the lawn, just to calm himself down.

He wonders yet again if this is how it feels to be an artist—using your hands and eyes but also thinking things through as you work, finding meaning in every little choice you make. He thinks of Zach wishing he could sing, how if he'd had that kind of talent, he'd want to do it all the time. That's how Max feels about working on his book. It rings all his bells. His face is stuck in a perpetual grin.

When his brain finally stops buzzing and he's breathing normally again, he goes back inside.

Mozelle is still bustling around, emptying drawers and cabinets, making decisions, filling and labeling boxes. She's been doing that all along, but Max has been too focused on his book to notice how much she's accomplished. Suddenly the end feels shockingly near. He can't kick this can down the road anymore—it's already there.

"Mozelle?" he says.

"What?" She's kneeling over a box with a roll of strapping tape in her hand.

"I've been thinking. I mean, I have an idea."

"Yes?" Maybe just a hint of impatience.

"If we stayed a little longer, till Mom gets back, then they could come up here. We could all be together. It'd be so cool."

Mozelle looks moderately stunned by this suggestion. "There's no room, Max."

"No, it'll work. I've got it all figured out. Mom and Dad could have your bedroom, you could sleep in mine—"

"Max, look around and tell me what you see."

"Boxes."

"Right. And the truck is scheduled for Monday morning. They'll take everything. Then we'll have to leave. The cabin will be empty and it's a long drive home."

"But couldn't you change it so the truck comes later? So Mom can see the cabin one last time?"

"Oh, Max!" She says it like he's totally breaking her

heart. "Use your head. We have no idea when Dory will be coming home. And when she does, she'll have to go back to work."

"Just a few more days!"

"We can't. I told the developer we'd vacate on Monday. It's all arranged. I'm so sorry."

"Can I take the Legos?" Rosie asks, totally out of the blue.

"Of course, sweetheart. Whatever you want."

"I want to stay longer," Max says.

"I know."

After lunch he takes his phone for another walk. Only this time he doesn't walk, he runs—blowing off steam, working off tension. It wears him out, but then, that's the point.

He can't imagine what he was thinking. It was perfectly obvious they'd be leaving soon. The cabin is a mess of boxes. Almost every surface is bare, most every drawer is empty. Even the kitchen is down to essentials. And somewhere in the nearest big town some contractor is lining up a bunch of cranes or backhoes or whatever it is you need to tear down buildings. Architects are drawing up plans for the fancy houses that will replace them.

Dumpsters and port-a-potties are on order. There's no stopping it now. Which means he'll only see Lila three more times. And he's nowhere near ready for it to be over.

Max has been so busy with his thoughts that he's missed his landmarks, blown right past them. Now he's solidly into the cell phone service zone—a miraculous three bars! Which would be super great if his phone weren't almost out of juice.

Still, with what he has left, he does a quick search. He has the feeling Henry will be easy.

And sure enough, right there on Wikipedia: Henry Aaron Rutledge, an artist famous for his monumental sculptures made of woven bamboo. His work is in the Museum of Modern Art and the Pompidou in Paris and a lot of other museums Max has never heard of.

Henry spent his early childhood in Japan, returning to the United States at the age of nine. He earned a BFA in sculpture from the Rhode Island School of Design, then went back to Japan to study with the great masters of bamboo weaving. He still lives there part-time.

He's thirty-six now. His face has become angular, with a rugged jaw like some old-time movie cowboy. He would be totally unrecognizable as the boy he once was were it not for the same pale hair and guarded expression.

Henry is married to a Japanese artist named Hideo—who is also famous for his works in bamboo, only his sculptures are small. Hideo has his own Wikipedia page, but Max doesn't have time to read it. His phone could shut down at any minute.

He's not surprised that Henry has become a famous artist. It's exactly what Max expected. But it amazes him that an abnormally shy and deeply private kid like Henry could end up falling in love and getting married. That he was actually able to open up and let another person into his life. It gives Max hope that he, too, might someday become a better version of himself.

Max looks at the picture of Henry again. It's a really amazing photo, but Henry didn't pose for it—no standing still, smiling for the camera. He was caught in motion, as if he'd been walking away when someone called his name and he turned, a busy man interrupted on his way to the next important thing. It's a remarkable portrait, a snapshot that's a dead-on perfect character study, one artist photographing another.

Max checks the battery icon. It looks like an empty bottle of red paint lying on its side, just a smear of color stuck to the bottom. There'll be no using it again unless they go back to Arnie's. Honestly, he'd walk there now, except that he hasn't brought his charger.

It hits him then, as a cold wave of gloom passes over his soul, that his entire life is running on red and about to shut down—their visit to the cabin, his time with Lila and his cool new friends, and the vastly smarter, more confident person he's been in the dream world. No more playing in the creek with his sister. No more forests and lakes and stars and the quiet of night. All of that will be gone.

Then he'll be back in New York, spending the dregs of his summer alone in the apartment with Rosie, while Dad works all day and Mom continues to float out there somewhere, doing her good deed, who knows for how long. Maybe for always.

He walks back slowly now, totally wiped out and seriously wondering if he's starting to lose it. One minute he's so excited it almost hurts. He's God's gift to the art world, full of ambition and plans.

Then the next he's gone manic, spinning impossible dreams and making ridiculous demands of Mozelle. He's going to bring his parents to the cabin! They will stay there till it happens! In an empty cabin with no food. And even as he's making these demands, he knows it's impossible. His mother isn't on her way home. She's been gone for ten days—*ten days*—and has only checked in once.

What are the chances she'll suddenly show up at just the perfect moment to play her part in Max's little fantasy?

And then, when Mozelle gently leads him back to reality, Max goes over the edge into a state of misery, where nothing good is even remotely possible and everything is just dark, dark, dark.

That is so totally not normal.

Chapter Fourteen

"I THINK I'M LOSING IT," he says.

They're standing on the road, about a third of the way down to the lake. Lila has her arms around him while he sobs into her hair. It would be way past embarrassing if he had the energy to care about making a fool of himself. Which he doesn't.

She holds him even tighter. It's like that day when he was five and he thought it would be cool to go down the slide headfirst, and they'd had to take him to the emergency room. His mom had held him in just this way. He'd even cried into her hair. Bled all over her jacket too.

Which, fortunately, is not the case this time.

Another minute passes, maybe two. When it drifts into his consciousness that this would make a really great picture for his book—actually two or three pictures from different angles to give the sense of what a *long* hug it was—he knows the crisis is over.

"I think I'm okay now," he says. He lets go, so she does too. "I think my personhood is reassembling itself."

"You sure?"

"Yeah. Thanks entirely to your magical healing powers. Too bad you're going into law, not medicine."

"I'm going into law?"

"Oops."

"You looked me up on that search thing?"

"The internet. Yeah, I did."

"Huh. That sounds so unlike me."

"Well, it's the kind of law where you defend poor people. So I suspect you're also poorly paid."

"Okay. Sounds a little less weird. Now do you think you can put one foot in front of the other and, like, move your body down the road?"

"I dunno. Probably. I'll give it a try."

He's definitely better by the time they arrive. There's still a buzzing in his brain, and the brain is not entirely functional, but he figures he can fake a bit of mindless conversation.

"Oh good," Lila says, pointing to the pier. "We're going across the lake. You'll like it, I promise." She waves energetically, like Robinson Crusoe trying to flag down a passing ship. Actually, Max has no idea whether that happens in the book or not, since he hasn't read it yet, but it stands to reason it would be. After all, it's a shipwreck story.

In this case, the boats are still tied up to the pier, though Zach and Amber are already seated in one of them, probably raring to go. Dee and Lenny are still discussing something, probably who sits where, while Rosie stands beside them in her straw hat and sunglasses. No tutu this time.

Lenny spots them and waves back.

"Do I look all splotchy and pathetic?"

"No. You look perfectly normal."

"You're not just saying that?"

"Your secret is safe, I promise."

They pick up the pace, maneuver their way through the cluster of teens, who are currently awake and actually talking to each other, till they reach the boats. By which time Lenny's in the second one, reaching up as Dee hands

Rosie down into his arms, then helping her get settled on one of the benches.

"What's with you guys?" Amber says. "Always late."

"Max and I were having a deep philosophical conversation. And, just to set the record straight, *you* were the last one yesterday."

"Yeah, okay. My bad."

"So who's rowing?"

"Lenny and Zach. But I'm rowing this one on the way back, just so you know." She addresses this pointedly to Zach.

"Got it," he says.

The others have already taken their places, and two more in either boat would be too many. So he and Lila will have to split up. And since Rosie is with Dee and Lenny, that's where Max should go.

As he steps in, the boat rocks wildly. There's a lot of yelling and he comes close to pitching overboard. But Lenny grabs him by the shirt and guides him onto a bench.

"Sorry," Max says with a sheepish grin. He has definitely not covered himself in glory. Yet strangely, he doesn't care. He's not sure why, but he suspects it has something to do with trust and character development.

Zach and Lenny cast off, and it soon becomes clear that they've done this many times before—all the fiddly stuff they know about the ropes and the oars. Max had always assumed that rowing a boat was a super-simple thing. You just get in and paddle away. And maybe that's true if you're not particular about the fine points of rowing—and don't much care whether you reach your destination or not.

But Lenny and Zach know exactly what they're doing, their form a perfect combo of power, precision, and grace. Max watches with a fair amount of guy envy—the way they lean forward, arms out, oars back, then drop the blades of the oars into the water at just the right angle and pull, muscles tight with the effort, leaning back, back, back in one fluid motion as the boat surges ahead.

It's a wondrous thing to watch. And he can't help wishing it was *him* up there, looking all manly and powerful. But it's not, so he decides to relax and enjoy the ride, the forward motion, the light sparkling off the water, the cool breeze, and the enormous grin on his sister's face.

Yet another entry to his growing list of Things He's Never Done Before: *riding in a rowboat.* (Previous entries: *wading in a creek, gazing at a night sky full of stars, walking through a forest, surviving without electricity,* and *swimming in a mountain lake.*)

Day One of the three he has left: at least it's going to be good.

There's no pier on the far side of the lake, just a shallow cove with a beach of sorts. Max wonders how they're going to land. Will they drop some secretly hidden anchor and swim? Then go hiking in soggy, wet shoes, *squelch, squelch, squelch*?

No, of course not.

As they approach the beach where the water is shallow, the bows of the boats grind against the sand and ease to a gradual stop. Zach and Lenny ship their oars. Then they all take off their shoes and toss them onto the beach. Because the next step is to jump out into knee-deep water—everyone except Rosie, who gets a piggyback ride from Lenny—and help haul the boats farther up on the shore. Not completely, just enough so they won't float away.

Which would definitely be a problem.

To be extra sure, they secure the lines to large rocks.

There follows a lot of foot wiping, tugging of socks over damp feet, tying of shoes. Then they head away from the lake, Zach in the lead, through a grassy section with small scrubby bushes, to the trailhead.

Max wonders if this counts as his first real hike. It's

way steeper and more technical than cutting through the woods, though both involve walking through a bunch of trees. But they could be two separate entries to his list if he's really going for the numbers—*taking a hike* and *walking through the woods*.

New experiences, left and right.

Yeah, he decides as the minutes pass, a hike is definitely different from a walk. It's pretty challenging in places, as in *straight up the mountain*, and it's not a smooth trail. You have to watch your step, or you'll twist an ankle or trip over rocks. Zach makes it look easy, but Max can feel his quads burning. Even his knees hurt.

He isn't aware that he's been huffing or groaning, but apparently he's made *some* kind of noise because Dee, who's just ahead of him on the trail, turns and stops.

"Can I show you a trick?" she says. "It's called the 'resting step.'"

Seriously? She's going to teach him how to walk?

"Sure," he says.

"So: You step forward like this, but before you take the next step you pause. Let the muscles recover for a nanosecond. Also it keeps you from pushing too hard." She demonstrates, taking three easy, purposeful steps up the trail, then turns and comes back down. She's smiling, like she's just given him a gift. "Also, concentrate on squeezing your glutes with every step. That'll engage your hamstrings."

This is too weird. He just stares.

"Really—your glutes and hamstrings are bigger than your quads. Use them to *push* yourself up the mountain, instead of pulling with your quads. You'll find it's a lot easier and much less painful."

"Wow, Dee, that's great!" Lila says, restoring Max's dignity to a small degree.

They practice it together, making jokes about their glutes, lurching up the trail like a pair of Frankenstein's monsters. But once they stop fooling around, they have to admit it's easier that way.

"Kind of a metaphor for life too," Dee adds. And when they both give her a slack-jawed stare: "Keep moving forward, but thoughtfully. Stop to rest from time and time. And use your strengths."

"That's awesome," Max says. Because it is.

At the summit there's an open space with a panoramic view. Across the lake they can see the compound. Or rather, they can see the cleared area with the ball field and playground. Everything else looks untouched. Here and there you can spot a bit of the road, but mostly it's just trees. The cabins blend in so perfectly they're almost invisible.

Such a light, respectful footprint on the land! Max feels unaccountably proud.

"From there"—Zach points to the stream that flows past Henry's structure—"all the way around as far as you can see, is a state park. The main entrances are way, way over on the other side. We came in the back door.

"Now if you look down and to the left, over there, see that open area? It's a campground. But nobody ever goes there because it's so far from the entrance. Which means you can have it all to yourself."

"You've stayed there?"

"We go every summer. My mom and dad and my brothers, we rent a motor boat and take it over here in the afternoon, then backpack into the campground and spend the night under the stars. It's totally great. It's not as developed as the others, but I like it way better."

Max has a sudden thought. "Zach—when you're there, sleeping under the stars—do you dream? I mean—"

"I know what you mean. So, yeah. Though it tends to be shorter than usual. The light wakes you up really early. 'Course, if you had a tent, it would be different, I guess."

"So the dreaming—it's not just at the compound?"

"We're not at the compound now, Max."

Good point.

"What if you drove to Millie's Crossing and stayed in a motel—assuming there was a motel, which I'm sure there isn't—would you dream there?" He's thinking that maybe the dreaming is like cellular coverage—you have it, have it, have it, until you've gone too far and then you don't.

"No clue. Never even thought about it."

Max, however, cannot stop thinking about it.

"So you have to carry all your stuff? Food and water and sleeping bags?"

"That's what backpacking is, Max."

He looks around him—at the trees and the lake. Imagines being here with his mom and dad and Rosie. He can't quite see Mozelle hiking in—but who knows? They could carry her stuff and Max could teach her the resting step. Of course they'd need a boat . . .

"Is there a way to drive in?" he asks. "To that particular campground down there?"

"Sure. There are roads to all the campgrounds. But you'd have to drive back to the highway, then all the way around to the other side of the park where the entrance is. It'd take hours and hours."

"But if you were coming directly from New York, not from the compound?"

"I guess that would work. Why not?"

"And you could drive all the way in and park at that camping spot, so you wouldn't have to carry everything. And you could bring tents and enough food to last days and days."

"Not as much fun that way, but yeah."

"Well, if you had a grandmother with you."

"Got it." He shrugs, because of course he doesn't actually get it, or not the big picture anyway.

Max turns to Lila. She's sitting in the stubbly grass, leaning against a tree, her eyes closed, the sun on her face. But she's awake and listening. He knows because she's smiling.

Chapter Fifteen

"WHEN YOU COME TO A STOPPING POINT, I have a project for you."

Max looks up from his book, bleary-eyed. He's been at it all morning, so deeply focused on his task, his grandmother's voice seems to pull him out of a heavy sleep, the kind where you want to move or speak but you can't because you're paralyzed.

He'd arrived at a crucial point. Having finished his cast of characters, it was time to actually tell his story. He'd already done "Max and Lila Meet Cute," but that was just a regular double-page spread. Now, with the chess game, there would be action. He'd already decided to break it up into a series of mini-scenes, with pictures in panels of varying shapes and sizes, and to keep it going for several pages. But this was something new for him, and he wasn't sure how to go about it.

He was sitting there worrying about maybe screwing it up, and that made him wonder if he could tear out any screwed-up pages without the whole book falling apart. And then he thought maybe he should plan it out really carefully before drawing anything. That's when he had his breakthrough.

He would work out the series in advance, not in pictures but in *words*. Like he was writing a screenplay. He'd describe it scene by scene: Long shot of the picnic table. Camera moves in to focus on Lenny, Dee, and Rosie. Close-up of the chessboard with Rosie's hand moving a piece. Close-up of Rosie's face, looking excited. Pull back as the soccer ball comes flying in.

He was amazed by how naturally the images revealed themselves when he started thinking like a movie director. Seriously, it took him five minutes. Even deciding the size of the panels was easy. Long shot of picnic table—a big horizontal panel, half a page. Close-up of Rosie's face—a square panel, smaller.

After that, it was like he was racing the clock, not

because it mattered how long it took but because the process was so all-consuming, and his mind was sprinting ahead so fast, he couldn't control it. He practically had to remind himself to breathe and to blink—definitely some sort of altered state, though hopefully not the kind that made Vincent van Gogh go crazy and cut off his ear.

So that's basically where Max is, mentally speaking, when Mozelle shuts down the pumping fire hose of creative thought with "When you come to a stopping point . . ."

And just like that, he sees that he has—come to a stopping point. He's standing on the cliff edge of exhaustion. "Sure," he says.

Meanwhile, Rosie has been drawing dragons. It's not clear what part they play in her story, but they're definitely cute, sort of like seals with bat wings and pointy tails that breathe fire or blow puffs of smoke. She's filled page after page with them, each with some slight variation—eyelashes, leopard spots, giant ears.

Rosie also looks up at Mozelle, a little cross-eyed with weariness. "What project?" she says.

"A farewell-to-the-cabin sort of project."

Max gives her a quizzical look. "How does that work, exactly?"

"Well, it has various elements, but the main one might

take a while, so I thought we could get a head start on it today."

This is something Mozelle likes to do—drag out a story till it makes you want to scream.

"Now comes the part where you tell us what it is."

"Yes, Max, I suppose you're right." At which point she brings out a pack of fat colored markers. Max had noticed her buying them at Arnie's, but he'd assumed they were for labeling boxes.

She tears off the plastic wrapping and drops the markers onto the table. Every color of the rainbow. "Shall I demonstrate?"

"Um, sure . . ."

She takes a blue marker and goes over to the bookshelf. The shelves themselves are stained wood, but the backs are painted white. On this white surface, she neatly prints:

GOOD BOOKS LIVED HERE

Rosie sucks in breath. She had once drawn with crayon on the wall of their apartment and you'd have thought she'd committed murder. Yet here was their grandmother going at the bookshelves with a marker. Did this mean it was okay?

Evidently. Because now Mozelle is drawing a bowl of pasta on the wall beside the kitchen door, complete with wavy lines above it to suggest that it's hot and smells delicious. Above the picture she creates an arch of lettering:

GOOD FOOD WAS COOKED IN THIS KITCHEN

Max is up now, a purple marker in his hand. He adds an arrow from the pasta bowl to the kitchen door. Just to be really clear, since no cooking took place in the living room.

"I don't think you can wash that off," Rosie says, still scandalized.

"Oh, sweetheart, we don't want to wash it off. We want our happy memories and good wishes to stay with this house for as long as it remains."

And with that Rosie starts to cry. Because the truth has finally hit her that the cabin will be demolished. Gone. Hauled off in pieces to a dump somewhere.

It's good that she hasn't imagined the rest of the story. Because Max has, and it breaks his heart—not just what will be torn down, but what will take its place. However nice the houses or green the lawns, they will never fit in with this beautiful place. They will ruin it.

The new people will jet around the lake in speedboats. They'll have loud parties on their decks. Drive over to the new Arnie's for an espresso and some premade city food. And in the evenings, they'll go inside and stream movies on their big-screen TVs. Or play games on their computers. Or mess with their phones.

The hillside will be filled with their lights and their noise, so they won't be able to see the stars or hear the wind in the trees.

And they won't even know what they're missing.

He wonders if their children will dream. Probably not, since there won't be the long, dark nights. No first and second sleep. So the dream world will empty out. And that will be the end of it.

Mozelle is drawing pictures of Max and Rosie now, wearing crowns and royal robes. She labels them Prince Maximillian and Princess Rosemond. And it's as if Mozelle had waved a magic wand because Rosie stops crying now, takes a couple of markers, and starts drawing dragons on the wall.

"What are they for?" Max asks. "The dragons?"

"To protect the cabin."

"Of course. Why didn't I think of that?"

"I don't know," Rosie says.

Max looks thoughtfully at the exterior walls, wondering if marker would show up against the dark wood of the exposed logs. Probably not, but it's worth a try. So he goes over to the couch, kneels on it, and writes in black marker:

LOG

And yeah, you can definitely see it if you're actively looking, but it's not even remotely as satisfying as writing on the white Sheetrocked walls. So he goes into his bedroom and, on the spot where the Chagall print hung before it was taken down and packed away, he draws a picture frame. Inside he draws a tree and a pretty rough version of the floating goat and violin-playing person. Above it, he writes:

THERE WAS A PICTURE HERE
DORY PICKED IT OUT

Above the dresser, bare now, he writes the names of all of his mom's books that he can remember. He uses different lettering for each one. It's pretty great when he's finished, like a really cool wallpaper design.

He goes back into the living room, gets some different colored markers, and drags a chair into his room. Plants it just inside the door frame and climbs up. Above the lintel he writes:

DOROTHEA GLICKMAN SLEPT HERE
SO DID HER SON, MAX

He returns the chair. Sits down. Admires what they've already done. "Mozelle," he says, "are we going back to Arnie's before we leave?"

"Yes, tomorrow. Why?"

"When we're finished, I think we should take pictures so Mom can see this. I think it would make her happy, don't you?"

"Yes, Max, that's a brilliant idea. But your phone is dead, am I correct?"

"Totally and completely."

"That problem can be solved."

"I'm glad to hear it. Do you mind if I decorate your bedroom?"

"I would be delighted."

The white wall dividing the kitchen from the bedroom is a perfect canvas. He slips off his shoes and climbs onto the bed, stands in front of the wall, and starts with a picture of Marvin.

Max was just seven when his grandfather died, but

he can tell you a thousand things about him. How Marvin was a little odd (in a really cool way) and was always coming up with this weird stuff to do. Like dressing up as the Statue of Liberty on the Fourth of July (draped in a bedsheet and wearing one of those green Styrofoam liberty crowns on his head) and dramatically reading the Declaration of Independence as printed in the *New York Times*.

Or that life-sized stuffed goose hand puppet he gave Max for his birthday. He could make it do all sorts of things, like peck at Max's head. He even made it sing. Well, Marvin did the singing, but the goose waved its head around in a singing kind of way—pointing its bill to the ceiling on the high notes, dipping down for the low ones.

Also, there was Marvin's laugh. It was really more like a deep chuckle, like anything he found to be funny was extremely enjoyable, and for some reason it made Max feel like they were sharing a secret joke together.

All those memories—yet Max can't quite remember Marvin's face. All that come to mind is a generic older man with white hair and horn-rimmed glasses. Which means his portrait won't be very good. But then, he's drawing on a wall with fat markers, so the bar's already set pretty low, artistically speaking. He does his best.

Beside Marvin he draws Mozelle, curly hair and

glasses. Both of them smiling. He knows it's corny, but he draws some red hearts floating in the air around them. They form a pattern that's really quite satisfying. He adds some little flying birds. Lovebirds.

Above it all he writes, in a curving arch like the one over the pasta bowl:

THE M&Ms FOREVER!!

Mozelle is standing in the doorway, watching him. "The M and Ms?" she says.

"That's what we used to call you. Like 'the M and Ms are coming over for dinner tonight.'"

"I never heard that. How clever." Then: "Thank you for drawing Marvin."

"Can I do word balloons?"

"I don't know. What would we be saying?"

"Will you trust me?"

"Of course."

So Max makes two of them, writing the words first, then putting the balloon around them after so it'll be a perfect fit. Marvin says:

GOODBYE, WONDERFUL CABIN
IN THE WOODS

And Mozelle says:

WE WERE
HAPPY HERE

"That's perfect, Max. And very true."

That night, as Max lies in the darkness thinking about the ending of things, a thin strip of light appears at the bottom of his bedroom door. It's totally quiet by then. Rosie's probably sound asleep and Mozelle must be feeling restless, so she's come out to the living room to read for a while.

He opens the door a crack to see. She's sitting on the couch by the light of a single lantern, turning the pages of his book. Which he'd forgotten to put away in the drawer. Which he left lying on the table instead. She looks up as he comes in.

"Hi," she whispers. She puts the book back on the coffee table and pats the space beside her on the couch, inviting him to sit. "I hope you don't mind. I was admiring the drawings in your book."

"That's okay. It's just a story I'm making up. Kind of like a graphic novel."

"Your drawings are incredible, Max. Very accomplished. I had no idea."

"Thanks. I had a really good art class at camp this summer."

"I know. And I think you should take more lessons. I'll mention it to your dad."

"That'd be cool." He gets the feeling she has something to say, besides how good he is at art. But she's taking her time, easing into it.

"I like the portraits. Especially the one of Henry."

"Yeah, that's my favorite too—because of the background. The darkness and the dramatic light."

"Exactly. It's painterly. It has mood, a sense of place."

A bright bloom of warmth rises in his chest. She really means it, he can tell.

"Did you know there's actually a famous artist named Henry Rutledge?"

"Um, no. Or I guess I must have heard it but didn't remember, then it just popped into my head."

"Maybe. Also, another portrait really struck me. The picture of 'Dee.'"

He blinks.

"She looks so much like your mother when she was that age! Here, let me show you."

Only then does he notice, also on the coffee table, a small photo album. "I'd forgotten about this. It's from her Polaroid summer. Mostly it was Dory taking the pictures.

But there are a few we took of her. Here, look. Don't you see the resemblance?"

"That's *Mom?*" he says.

"The hair, I know—it was awful! But she was going through that phase where she just *had* to look like everybody else, and that meant having long, straight hair. Poor bubby, born with all those crazy curls! I finally gave in and let her have it straightened. And then she went to the drugstore and bought this black hair dye and, omigod, she looked just like Morticia in those Charles Addams cartoons! But I just kept telling myself, *This, too, will pass.* And finally it did."

Max is only half listening. He's still staring at the girl in the faded Polaroid. Not only does she look exactly like Dee, he's now noticed something else: the necklace Dee always wears, a gold chain with a small red stone. It's in the photo. It's in his drawing. He feels chills running down his arms.

"And this is so strange," Mozelle says. "I almost don't dare mention it."

Max is having trouble breathing—and there's more?

"That's what we used to call your mom back then. Everybody else called her Dory or Dorothea, but Marvin and I called her Dee."

When his eyes go wide, she grins. "I know! It's like

something out of *The Twilight Zone*." Then she does this little song thing, like *dee-dee dee-dee, dee-dee dee-dee*. Probably the theme music from the show. Which is really ancient and Max has never seen it, but he knows it's famous, an icon of science fiction, and people still make that *dee-dee dee-dee* sound when they're describing something creepy.

"Yeah," he says, his voice flat. "That's so weird."

He sits there for a while, his head down, flipping through pages of faded nature photos, waiting for the storm in his brain to subside. Finally, when he can breathe more or less normally, he sets the album back on the table, casually picks up his book, says good night, and goes to bed.

Chapter Sixteen

"OF COURSE, YOU KNOW WHAT THIS MEANS," Lila says.

"The Old Friend. It has to be Lenny."

"It absolutely does. They've always been close. And Lenny's just the sort of person to take on the world for a cause. Remember what they both said about making sacrifices?"

He nods. "I was thinking about that last night, after I found out. Something in your question, I don't remember the exact words, but it made the point that the sacrifice would be for yourself but also for others. And I knew you were thinking about Mom when you wrote it. Because it's been a sacrifice for us too. And, you know, we weren't consulted. And my grandmother's old. And Rosie's so little."

"I know. And you can unload all that when it's over. But for now, let's concentrate on finding her."

"Yeah. I'll call my dad in the morning so he can do an internet search. But I'll need Lenny's full name."

"Want me to ask him?"

"How would you do that?"

"Well, I'll tell him about the search thing."

"Internet search."

"Right."

"Which you do on a computer. Or you can do it on a phone, but let's not go there. Keep it simple."

"I think that'll really interest him," she says. "The technology, the fact that you can look him up and learn all about his future life. I'll tell him you already did a search on me and that I become a lawyer."

"I also looked up Henry. He's a super-famous artist."

"Really? Wow! I'll tell him that too. Then I'll say you think he's such an interesting person, he'll probably grow up to, I don't know, cure cancer or something. And since you're leaving soon and won't be coming back, you would really like to know how he turns out. I won't mention the bit about camping across the lake. It's a better story if you're leaving for good."

He does a thing with his hands, hardly knows why he's doing it. A gesture of impatience that says, *I can't talk about that right now!* Then he runs his hands over his face, as if wiping away his expression.

"Just do it in private," he says with a sigh. "Because if you ask Lenny when the others are around, they might start telling their names too. Then Rosie will figure out about Dee and . . . you know, basically your full-bore, world-crushing disaster!"

"I won't let that happen, I promise. I'll be super careful and I'll let Lenny know that it's a very secret thing. He'll respect that. But—just thinking ahead here—he'll wonder where you are and why *I'm* the one who's asking. Actually, they'll all want to know what's up—you know, me without you. What should I say?"

"I don't know. But I definitely can't be with them right now. I'm not sure I should see Dee at all. Just think what's already happened. She met me and Rosie, has only known us for a week—yet years later she names her kids Max and Rosie? So what if we *hadn't* come here? Would we be George and Martha now? Or not even be here at all? It feels like a really dangerous thing to mess with."

"Maybe you can just see them briefly, to tell them all goodbye? No emotion, no big deal."

"Okay, good idea. I'll make it the least memorable farewell in history. But, you know, not today."

"Then here's what we'll do. You go to Henry's place. Help him work on his structure like he said we could. I'll tell them you're taking a last look around, since you'll be leaving and all, but they'll see you tomorrow for sure. Then I'll wait for the right moment to ask Lenny. And once I have his name, I'll join you at Henry's."

"You'll be careful?"

"Absolutely."

Henry isn't there yet, so Max crawls into the structure to wait. He stretches out, his head resting on his arms, and gazes out through the woven walls at the tops of the trees, shimmering bright and dark in the sunlight and shadow. A wave of ease washes over him. His muscles go slack; his mind is still. It's like that last waking moment just before you fall asleep.

Maybe that's why they call it falling. It's all about letting go.

He's not sure how long he's been there when some inner sense detects a subtle change. The birds have stopped calling. There's just this deep silence, broken only by the constant rush of the running stream. He can see it in his mind's eye—Henry standing a few yards away in a shaft of sunlight, the canvas bag in his hand, watching. Like the picture in his book.

He sits up. Turns. "I was waiting for you," he says. "You said I could help if I wanted."

Henry comes closer, sets down his bag. "Okay."

"But can I ask you something important first?"

Henry's silence feels like a yes.

"This place—don't you feel totally different when you're here? It's just so amazingly calm and peaceful, right? And I wonder if you picked this spot because of that."

"Yes. I made a study of the phenomenon, and it's more pronounced here than anywhere else. I believe this to be the center of the force."

"Like in *Star Wars*?"

"No. That's fiction. This is real. It's what causes us to dream together, regardless of our positions in time."

Oh. *That* force.

"And the center is right here?" Max plants his hand on the ground inside the structure.

"No. It's strongest over there." He points to a large, sloping boulder in the middle of the stream. "But I can't build in the water. And the force seems to flow under the ground and come out over there, the way the stream flows into the lake."

It occurs to Max that Henry, in addition to being both talented and unusual, might also be a little bit off his rocker. On the other hand, Max has experienced it himself, the strange, healing power of the place. And also . . . the dreams. He figures, why not this too?

"And the structure—what do you call it?"

"I don't call it anything."

"But what's it for, exactly? A shelter? A clubhouse?"

"I hope to concentrate the force in an enclosed space. Then maybe I can understand it."

"Concentrate it here, inside the structure?" It doesn't look like it could concentrate anything.

"The walls will have to be very tight." He touches a section where he's already started weaving in the vines. "Solid, like this. But it's slow work. I won't finish it this year."

"I'll be glad to help if you'll show me what to do."

"Okay." He squats down, opens the bag, and lays out his tools on a strip of white cloth. Then he goes over to the stream and raises one of the rocks that hold the vines in place, pulls out a handful, shifts the rock back. He uses a curved blade to trim them at both ends.

"What are those?" Max has crawled out of the structure now.

"Blackberry vines."

"But they don't look—"

"That's because I've stripped off the thorns and the outer skin. It makes them smooth and light in color, instead of dark." He takes one over to the structure and picks up where he left off the day before.

Max watches Henry's hands as they weave the vine neatly in and out through the open spaces in the wicker frame. When he's done, he uses the side of a screwdriver to press the new vine hard against its neighbor. "Like this," he says, handing Max the screwdriver and a couple of vines. "Tight."

"You don't need it?"

"I have other tools that will work just as well."

That's the last thing Henry says for maybe half an hour. They work together wordlessly, finding a rhythm, concentrating on what they're doing with their hands. Every now and then Henry comes over and stands behind him. But there's never a correction, so Max figures he's doing it right.

It reminds him a little of working on his book, the deep concentration on each stroke of the pencil. Except the weaving is more abstract and mechanical.

Or, no. *Mechanical* isn't the right word. That suggests a machinelike perfection, everything straight and even, nothing out of line. And that's definitely not how this is at all. Because the wicker frame, built of branches that grew in irregular ways, makes it impossible to achieve a perfect surface. And that's why it's so beautiful. The natural variations in the way the vines line up give it texture and character.

And the vines themselves, being smooth and pale, take on a sheen as they dry. When the sun hits them at the right angle, they glow like silver. He wonders if Henry planned it that way. If, even now, when he's still just a kid, he wants to honor his purpose with a beautiful work of art.

Max takes a step back to evaluate his work, a strip maybe ten inches wide and two feet high. He thinks it looks pretty good. "Is it okay?" he says, breaking the silence.

"Yes. Your technique is very exacting."

He sounds like a thirty-year-old engineer inhabiting the body of a boy.

"So," Max says, now that they're talking again, "I'm just curious—what will you do about the door and the window? If you want it to be tight and enclosed and all . . ."

"I will make a hinged door to close off the entrance. And the round hole is not a window. There'll be an extension that arches over the stream and rests on the boulder. I'm still considering the design."

"What's the extension for?"

"To connect with the origin."

Max imagines a wicker tube, like the hose of some primitive vacuum cleaner, sucking an invisible force out of a rock and into a wicker bag. The whole concept is so bizarre it makes him want to laugh. But he suspects Henry doesn't have much of a sense of humor. And besides, with all the impossible things he's already accepted as true, why not a rock that's the source of the force?

"When it's finished, what will you do?"

"Go inside, close the door, and wait."

"For what?"

"That's the question, isn't it?"

He hears her before he sees her, racing up the path like a bear is in hot pursuit. "You're still here," she says, leaning over, hands on knees, gasping for breath.

"Where did you think I'd be?"

"Gone. You know. Awake. In your bed. At the cabin."

"Has it really been that long?"

"Yes! But it was hard to get Lenny away from the group. First they were swimming, and that took forever, and when they finally came out of the water they were all together, talking. I couldn't think of a way."

"But you did?"

Max is aware that Henry is listening. He stands there, frozen in his work. Max decides this isn't a problem. If he had to trust someone to overhear a secret and not go spreading it around, Henry would be right at the top of his list.

"Yeah. I asked if I could 'consult' with him about something. Of course eyebrows went up, but nobody asked. They just watched us as we went off for our little walk-and-talk, out of earshot. But they were definitely curious, Lenny most of all."

"Are we building up the suspense here, or what?"

"Sorry. So I started in with the bit about your leaving, and how you were really sad about it and needed some time alone. I also mentioned Henry, said you wanted to tell him goodbye. And of course Lenny was interested in that too. Which, you know, dragged things out. I didn't say anything about the structure, though." She says this to Henry, who still hasn't moved. "I wasn't sure if you'd want other people to know."

When Henry doesn't respond, she turns back to Max. "So I reminded him that you were dreaming from a much later point in time, and your world is full of all this cool technology. Like there are these computers—and he said, 'I know what a computer is.' And I said, 'Yeah, me too, but these are *personal* computers, like *everybody* has one at home. And there's this thing called the internet that has *all the information in the world*, like an encyclopedia on steroids, and all you have to do is type a question into the computer and you'll get the answer on your screen.' And he's like, wow!"

"Lila?"

"What?"

"If at any point either of us starts to fade away, can you cut to the chase and give me the name? So I won't have to wait till tomorrow?"

"Leonard Eugene Russo. From Brooklyn."

Max repeats it twice. Then finds a twig and writes it in the dirt. Two paths to memory retention. Belt and suspenders.

"Thank you, Lila. You can continue."

"I don't have to. I didn't mean to run on and on."

"No, seriously. It's entertaining. Besides, I need to know what you told him so I can figure out what I'm going to say to them tomorrow. Get our stories straight. So far, I'm sad about leaving, I'm saying goodbye to Henry, and I may need to correct some of that stuff about the internet."

"Well, anyway. I said you'd asked me for my full name so you could do a search and find out what happened to me in the future. And he was like, 'He can *do* that?' And I'm like, 'Yes! And I become a lawyer!'"

"Public defender."

"Right. And then I mentioned . . ." She glances over at Henry, then at Max.

"Henry," Max says. "I hope you don't mind. I looked you up on the internet too. Remember I told you I had the feeling you were going to be a famous artist? Well, I was right. You make these huge bamboo sculptures. There's one in the Museum of Modern Art."

Henry finally lowers his hands. Blinks. Runs it through his mind, the idea that Max can reveal his future.

"And you're happy, too, not just famous. You're married to another artist and you live all over the world. You have a great life."

Henry looks away, but Max is pretty sure he isn't upset. It's just the way he is. "That must make you feel very powerful," Henry says. "To see the future."

"Well, it's not the future to me, it's my regular world. And in my time, they're just things that have already happened. So there's no power to it, just a matter of looking it up."

"Thank you for telling me." He's still not looking at Max, but he seems strangely relieved now, ready to go back to weaving vines.

And still listening.

"So you told him I'd looked up Henry too?"

"Yes. So he wouldn't think he was the only one. Besides me, but I'm in a special category."

"You definitely are. Your posture and all."

"And boldness. So, after that, I said pretty much what you told me—that you think he'll accomplish great things and you're curious to know how it all turns out. So he told me his name and asked if you would give him a report tomorrow. And that really threw me. I said I didn't know, but I'd ask."

"Did you tell him not to mention it to the others?"

"Yes. I made a huge point of it, said it twice. So we decided he'd tell the group our talk was just about you, and how you're kind of depressed about leaving and all. It's not a great story—I mean, why would I come down and discuss that privately with . . ."

Her voice has slowed. Now it stops. Her eyes seem vacant, unfocused. And her whole self seems less substantial. He reaches out and touches her arm. It feels insubstantial too. And then, in a matter of seconds, she has faded completely away.

He turns to Henry, who meets his eyes directly for the very first time.

"It's always so unsettling," Henry says.

Chapter Seventeen

MAX HEADS STRAIGHT FOR THE LIVING ROOM, still in his T-shirt and boxers, grabs a pen and a yellow pad, and writes down the name. Tears off the sheet of paper. Then hurries back to his room to get dressed.

"What was *that* about?" Mozelle asks when he comes out the second time.

"Something I need to remember. What time is it?"

"Seven fifteen. There's banana bread in the oven."

"I need to call Dad first."

"Why don't we wait till Rosie gets up?"

"We can call again later. I have to talk to him right now." It's not a question. He's not asking permission. He just grabs the phone and heads out the door.

"Dad?" he says, doing his best to sound calmer than he feels. "Did I wake you up?"

It's Sunday, Max realizes, so his dad had probably planned to sleep in.

"I was *thinking* about getting up. Considering the possibility."

"Sorry, but this is really important."

"Okay, Max. I'm listening."

"When Mom used to come here, back when she was my age, she had a very close friend. I think he's our guy."

"How did you hear about this?"

"It's a long story. But you need to look him up right away. His name is Leonard Eugene Russo. He lived in Brooklyn at the time, in case that helps."

"Okay. I'll get right on it. So are you mostly packed up? Ready to roll tomorrow?"

"Yeah. But Dad—please look him up right now. Then call me back and tell me what you find."

"Whoa, okay. Can I make some coffee first?"

Max is ready to scream with frustration. "Sure. But I'm serious, Dad. I really, really think he's the one."

"Well, I hope you're right. I'll get back to you when I have anything to tell."

"You got the name?"

"Leonard Eugene Russo from Brooklyn. I'm on it."

Max walks back to the porch, his heart still pounding. Unrolls the solar charger in a sunny spot and plugs in the phone. Then he sits on the steps for a couple of minutes, trying to bring himself down from an adrenaline high.

It was hard turning it over to Dad. Max would so much rather do the search himself. But for now, all he can do is wait.

After breakfast, they call Dad again. It's part of their routine now and Rosie finds it comforting, even when no one has anything to say. Max half resents this because it means taking Dad away from the search for Lenny. On the other hand, he might have already found something. Maybe not enough to justify a call, but Max would still like to hear it.

"Hi, Daddy," Rosie says.

Silence.

"Yeah, we had banana bread. We're all out of orange juice."

Silence.

"Uh-huh. We found these magic rocks. We're bringing them home."

Silence.

"Okay. See you tomorrow." Then: "Here, Daddy wants to talk to you."

It's all Max can do not to snatch the phone out of her hand. "Hi," he says.

"Well, it's possible I have the wrong Leonard Russo, but he's four years younger than Mom, so it seems unlikely that they'd be friends. I think maybe—"

"Trust me, they were. He's the guy. What else?"

"Odds and ends. I haven't started to dig deep yet. I was put off by the age difference. Four years is a big gap when you're that age. It's the same as you and Rosie."

"I know, Dad. But I'm *begging* you to trust me. It's him. You'll see."

"Well, I'll do what I can. And if something encouraging turns up, I can call our office's data guru and ask him to help as a favor to me. He's a lot better at this stuff than I am. He'll find things I would miss."

"And you'll let me know?"

"Of course."

"Trust me."

"Okay. Now let me talk to Mozelle."

* * *

They spend the morning doing their final packing, leaving only the essentials, then strategically loading the car. The cabin has been completely transformed. No longer a cozy fantasy of frontier America, it now looks like a modern art gallery that's currently being used as a storage unit.

The kitchen is barely functional. The pots and pans, dishes and silverware, and anything else worth giving away have been boxed and piled on top of other boxes, waiting for the movers. Plastic bags full of trash are lined up outside the back door. The truck will take them to a landfill on its way to the Goodwill drop-off.

It's typical of Mozelle that she hired a truck and driver to carry their stuff away when she could have saved the money and the effort by just walking out the door, leaving all the contents behind. The destruction crew would demolish it along with the cabin and haul away the pieces for free.

But she's not that kind of person. Instead, she's hired movers and is giving a party for the house.

By one o'clock, when they've pretty much done what they can, they drive to Arnie's to charge Max's phone. They also buy some snack food for lunch and a frozen pizza for dinner. They'll cut the pizza with the only knife Mozelle has not yet packed and eat it with their hands off paper towels. For breakfast they'll finish the last of the banana bread.

You know you're really leaving a place when you let the food run out.

They're on their way back from Arnie's when Dad calls.

"We've found something promising," he says.

"We?"

"Marcus is helping. Our data guru."

"Yeah. I remember."

"So, Leonard Russo has a master's degree from MIT in bioinformatics." He pauses, like something's coming. "And he's senior data manager at Lauette Pharmaceuticals in Watertown, New Jersey. I looked up the job description. Pretty interesting. He's responsible for the 'review and management of all clinical data supporting the Lauette portfolio.' I assume that means he reviews all the clinical studies on their new products."

"That fits, doesn't it? The whistleblower thing?"

Mozelle is slowing down now, pulling over.

"Yes, it does. It's making me forget the four-year age difference. But there's more. His job includes 'developing and maintaining key data management deliverables used to collect, review, monitor, and ensure the integrity of clinical data.' It sounds like Leonard Russo has access to *everything*—not just the data but the security that protects it and the systems that organize it. So if Lauette is cutting corners or trimming their data—"

"Did I mention he has a photographic memory? He's especially good with numbers."

They're stopped now, the engine is off, and Mozelle has turned in her seat, staring at Max.

"No, you did *not* mention that. But it would certainly be a handy talent for spotting discrepancies."

"So now what?"

"I've told Marcus the situation, just between us. Now he's really motivated to find this guy. We know he owns a house in Watertown, but if he's absconded with the company secrets, he's definitely not going to be there, waiting for the security people to show up at his door. Which explains why he's currently in Maryland."

"But where exactly?"

"Edgewater. Remember? The Starbucks?"

"Yeah, I know. But it's not like you can go door-to-door through the whole town."

"Marcus is still looking. We'll see what he turns up."

"Okay. Thanks."

"And Max?

"Yeah?"

"Good work."

The car is still on the side of the road. Mozelle is still staring at Max. From the back seat Rosie says, "What was that about?"

"Dad has a lead on the Old Friend."

"Really?" Mozelle says. Her gaze is so intense he has to look away.

"Yes. And he works for a drug company in the kind of job that gives him access to all their data, and security, and everything."

"And he has a photographic memory." There's this undertone in her voice and expression that says, *We'll be discussing this later.*

"I thought there was no such thing," Rosie says.

"Just a figure of speech," Mozelle says. "But it does fit our theory nicely. Something medical, full access to all the data, a strong memory, good at numbers."

"Yes," Max says. "It does."

He knows what she's going to say when they get back to the cabin, the questions she's going to ask. So somehow, between now and then, he needs to come up with a story. It won't be a good one—that's not even remotely possible. He'd settle for marginally plausible.

And still he comes up with nothing.

They park in back of the cabin, with its jarring parade of white plastic garbage bags. They carry in the food. While Mozelle is putting the pizza in the icebox, Max grabs a granola bar and makes his escape. Into his room, shuts the door.

This doesn't last for long.

"Rosie," Mozelle says, her voice a bit louder than necessary, plainly meant for Max to hear, "why don't you get some markers and decorate the bathroom. It's feeling neglected."

"I could draw Arnie."

"Absolutely, you should."

"And maybe a bear."

"Good idea. A very peaceful, friendly bear who keeps to himself."

Then Mozelle knocks on his door.

"Max, would you mind helping me rearrange some of the boxes in the car?"

She would have made a terrific undercover agent. The whole performance is flawless. And there is no way Max can refuse.

Outside, she takes his arm and guides him away from the house—not around front, but through the trees in back of the cabin, where Max has never been. There's a fair amount of tramping through leaves and stepping over branches. But this is not a random walk. Mozelle knows exactly where they're going.

It turns out to be a fallen tree, now bare of leaves and most of its branches. It's about the height of a park bench. A private, comfortable place to talk.

She sits fairly close to him, angled in his direction, then reaches out to lay a hand on his arm. It's gentle but firm, somewhere between *Poor thing!* and *Boy, are you in trouble!*

"I need you to tell me the truth," she says. "I know you'd rather not because you're afraid I won't believe you. But do it anyway."

And he wonders—does she already know? Has she always known?

So he tells her the truth, all of it, and she doesn't interrupt. When he's finished, she gives him a minute of silence in case there's something else. But there's not. He's spilled everything he's got.

"So you feel good about Lenny? You consider him a sane and moral person, not a danger to Dory?"

"Yes!" he says. "Totally. That's the whole point. He was the obvious one *because* he's the kind of person Mom would like and trust. Someone she'd make an effort to stay in touch with in the real world, even though they were different ages. He's genius-brilliant. And he's funny and interesting. And they both made this big point about helping others, doing the right thing, even if it meant making sacrifices. He would never be a danger to her."

Mozelle seems impressed by this impassioned speech. She squeezes his arm and finally lets go.

"Mozelle, can I ask—"

"Anything."

"Last night, when you were looking at my book?"

"Yes."

"That's when I figured it out. And once I realized Dee was Mom, I knew Lenny had to be the friend."

She nods.

"But you already knew, didn't you? About the dreams?"

"Dory told me."

"And you believed her?"

"I wasn't sure. She had a very active imagination. But it had such a sense of reality about it, the things she told me. And she was never the kind of kid who had imaginary friends. Just, you know, creative."

He has the feeling there's more.

"And then when I saw the pictures in your book, well, I knew it had to be true."

"What did she tell you, about the dreams?"

"Not a lot, mostly how much she liked her friends from the dreams. But she particularly mentioned this little girl named Rosie, and how they adored each other. She said it gave her a sense of what it must be like to be a mom, that looking after Rosie made her feel 'warm inside.' And she asked if that was the way I felt about her. Well, that's not the sort of thing a mother forgets. I said yes, that's exactly how it feels. When Rosie didn't come back the next summer, she took it very hard."

"Do you think Mom will figure it out? That her Rosie back then is her Rosie now? I mean, once she knows we've been at the cabin, she'll guess that we've been dreaming. Won't she put it all together?"

"Probably."

Her hand is on his arm again. She's studying his expression. "But even if she does remember, the world won't stop turning. You were important to her then, you're important to her now. Maybe you should just leave it at that."

"But think about it! By coming here, and meeting us in her dreams, we changed her past. Until this week, we weren't in her dreams, and if we'd stayed in New York, we never would be. So the fact that we're named Max and Rosie means that just this week we changed our own past, and maybe our future too."

"It kind of spirals, doesn't it, a series of alternate versions."

"Yeah. And it's terrifying. Like—where did you meet Marvin?"

"At a party."

"Okay, so what if you hadn't gone to that party? Then your whole life would have been different. You'd have married someone else and maybe lived somewhere else and you would have had different kids—"

"I get it, Max. But let's suppose Dory and I had cleared out the cabin earlier, *before* she got the call from Lenny, so you and Rosie were never here, and never in her dreams. Would that change anything important? Wouldn't she still have met and married your father and had the same two children, a boy and a girl? You'd have different names, but that's about all. She'd have a few different memories. But nothing substantial would be altered."

"Yeah, I guess."

"And the version you have now, it's good, right? Whatever has changed from some other reality, this is the one you have now. And her relationship with Lenny—that was already there. She would have gone off to help him anyway."

He nods. It makes sense.

"On the other hand—I think you'll like this: if you *hadn't* come here, you wouldn't have figured out Lenny was the friend. And I have the feeling that things will turn out better for them because you *were* here—and made the effort to figure it all out and get Lenny's name so you could tell your dad. So if you interrupted the spiral and sent it off on a different course, it was better than if you hadn't. Can't you just accept that? This is the reality we have?"

He nods. Yes, he can. He feels immensely better.

"One more thing?" he says.

"Okay."

"When you invited us to the cabin so we could get away from New York—were you hoping that maybe this would happen? Is that why you wanted us to come? Because the Old Friend might be someone Mom knew from her dreams?"

She closes her eyes and sighs. "It did occur to me, yes. But I also knew it would help you and Rosie to spend some time here. I rather think it has."

"Yeah. I'll miss it. I hate that we can't come back."

They let a respectful silence pass. Rest in peace, cute little cabin in the woods, where you can hear the wind in the pines and see a billion stars at night.

"So. We okay?"

"Yes."

"And you're satisfied with our arrangement of the boxes in the car?"

"The boxes? Oh. Right. Definitely. A big improvement."

The call comes in late, after they've all gone to bed. Max beats Mozelle to the phone, answers on the third ring. He holds it out so both of them can hear.

"We have our man," Dad says.

"What did you find?"

"It was Marcus's doing. Turns out Leonard Russo inherited a house from his aunt a couple of years ago. It's in Edgewater, Maryland, a stone's throw from the Starbucks where Dory sent her message. I'm flying to Baltimore tomorrow morning, get in around ten. Then I'll rent a car and drive to the house."

"And you have all the information about the lawyer and stuff?"

"Yes."

"Then what?"

"I've spoken with the attorney. He's one of the top guys in whistleblower law. I gave him what little information I have—a potential major pharmaceuticals case with a lot of documentation. He's definitely interested. My plan—assuming Mr. Russo will listen to reason—is to drive them to Pennsylvania tomorrow and meet with the attorney. It'll probably be safer there anyway. If Marcus could find the Edgewater house, the Lauette people can find it too. Maybe they already have."

It feels like a spy movie. Or a mob movie. Hide the witness in a safe house.

"What about Mom?"

"We may need to stay an extra night, make sure everything's set. But assuming the attorney is sold on the case, she won't need to be in the picture anymore. They'll bring in experts to analyze the data. Mom will probably want to want to talk them through it, though, give them a heads-up, point out the most glaring offenses. But if there're more, they'll find it."

The way Dad describes it, everything is settled, wrapped up, easy—the part between his flying to Baltimore and meeting with the lawyer just a formality.

But Max is trying to picture it. Dad pulling up in front of the Edgewater house. The curtains drawn, no car in the driveway, looks like an empty house. He walks up to the front door and knocks. And of course nobody answers. Why would they? No one knows about the house in Maryland—or wouldn't unless they'd searched pretty hard. And who would be searching besides Lauette security?

"What if they don't let you in? Don't even answer the door? I mean, they're hiding, right? Being super careful?"

"Don't worry. When Dory hears my voice, she'll open the door."

"But what if she's somewhere else—in the bathroom or down in the basement going through all that data? So it's just Lenny and he doesn't trust you."

"Let's not try to dredge up all the possible things that could go wrong. I'll identify myself. He knows about Dory's family. He'll let me in."

"I hope so."

"Think positive thoughts, Max. With any luck, the next call you get will be from Mom."

Chapter Eighteen

MAX IS ALONE WITH the stars for the final time. He's come out here every night between his first and second sleeps, and he can't bear to think he'll never have this experience again: the cool air on his arms and legs, the lumpy ground under his back. Just Max, by himself, gazing out into the universe and thinking how enormous it is, beyond his mind's ability to conceive it, going on and on for ever and ever, an endless expanse of space and time.

He will put this in his book because it's been so important to him. But not the dazzling star-filled sky—he wouldn't even dare to try. But he could draw himself, just a boy shape stretched out on the dark ground, softly lit by the stars. What the boy sees—and has seen for seven nights—will have to live on in his mind.

He promises himself that someday he will see the stars again like this. When that will be, or where, he doesn't know—but probably someplace wild and far away. The Kalahari Desert. Antarctica. The top of some great mountain. Till he finds that place, he'll remember this one. This sky, the way it makes him feel—incredibly small, more than a little afraid, and grateful.

As always—except for that first day, of course—Lila is already there, waiting for him when he falls into his dream.

"You're very dependable," he says.

"When it matters, I am." She gives him a laser look, eyes widened, brows raised.

"We found the house where they're staying. Dad's flying down there this morning. I think it's going to be okay."

"You're welcome."

"Um, thank you?"

She smiles.

"Also, my grandmother knows—about the dreaming. And that Dee is Dory and I've been hanging out with her, only we're weirdly the same age. Apparently, Mom told her about the dreams years ago. Mostly how much she loved being with Rosie."

"And she's okay with it, your grandmother?"

"Yeah. She basically told me to lighten up, just go with it. It'll be fine."

"Big day, huh?"

"Also—"

"There's more?"

"My grandmother gave us markers and we went all around the cabin drawing on the walls and writing about the good stuff that had happened there. Saying goodbye to the house and all the happy memories."

"Well, that's pretty much the greatest thing you've ever told me."

"There are lots of dragons and a few bears."

"Rosie's contribution?"

"How did you guess?"

"I'm super smart. Speaking of which, want to go see Henry?"

They're waiting in the structure when he arrives. It strikes Max, as Henry crawls in to join them, how much he's changed in just a couple of days. Like some wild creature that's been tamed through gentle kindness and respect.

For some reason, Max finds this thrilling. Whenever their eyes meet, however briefly, it feels like a triumph.

"Last day," Henry says, stating a fact.

"Yeah, sadly."

"You can help me again if you want."

"We do. And we will. But I've thought of something even better. It's your decision, of course."

A moment of silence. Lila and Henry both staring at him.

"So, what would you think if some of our friends came to help? You've met Lenny, right?"

He nods.

"He's tall, so he could help with the high parts that are hard to reach. And there's Dee—you'll like her. She's an artist, too, like you. She does these incredible drawings of plants. I think she'd be very careful in her work, do the weaving the way you want, neat and tight. The others are Amber and Zach. They could help with stuff like cutting and stripping the blackberry vines. It would go much faster that way. You might even be able to finish it this summer."

Now it's Max's turn to wait while Henry considers his proposal.

When a minute has passed with no response but a few thoughtful blinks, Max tries again. "You can say no. It was just a thought. But I'm sure they'd really like to help."

Max tells himself to shut up now, he's pushing too hard. Henry's not a hang-with-the-group sort of person. On the other hand, he's accepted Max and Lila, seems to feel comfortable with them now, and that was totally unexpected. . . .

"Sure. If they want to."

"Really? Great! I'll ask them."

"Okay," he says. And with that he crawls out, opens the canvas bag, and lays out his tools. Pulls a handful of vines from the stream and goes to work.

The group is over by the boulders again. Zach is skipping stones into the lake, getting three or four bounces before they sink. Rosie and Dee are making flower crowns. Amber's wading in the shallows. And Lenny isn't doing anything, just looking around, which is why he's the first to spot them. He waves and shouts. Then the rest of them turn to look.

From their anxious expressions, you'd think Max had just arisen from his deathbed. Apparently Lila had overdone it with all that business about poor Max, who is so upset about leaving he's gone off into the woods alone to deal with his grief.

Max waves back and grins, doing his best to look like a person who is not having a mental breakdown. Apparently, he's successful in this. The relief is visible on their faces.

"Look what I made!" Rosie says, holding up a string of tangled dandelions. She's totally in the moment, happy as a super-cute clam. Is it possible she doesn't remember that this is her last day? That in a matter of hours they'll be leaving the compound and she'll never see Dee again—or at least not the Dee who is sitting beside her now, making a beautifully crafted flower crown that Rosie will soon be wearing?

When it does finally dawn on her, will she have an old-fashioned Rosie meltdown? Go back to clutching Fluffy Rabbit and acting like a toddler? Somehow he doesn't think so. She's crossed a line this past week, into a better place.

Really, if Max is honest, they both have.

He chooses his boulder seat strategically, next to Lila and not facing Dee. "I was just saying goodbye to Henry."

"I didn't know you were friends," Dee says.

"Yeah, actually. It's kind of a new thing. But while I was there I got this really awesome idea."

Zach stops skipping stones. Even Rosie looks up.

"Henry's building this structure in the woods—in a clearing beside that stream over there. He let us help him work on it yesterday."

"What kind of structure?" Lenny asks.

"Kind of a huge basket, shaped like an igloo, made out of woven branches and vines. He's very technical about it, knows exactly what he's doing. And it's weirdly beautiful. Anyway, my thought was, you could come help too. It's fun, and with everyone working together, it won't take him so long to finish."

"Are you sure he'd be okay with that?" Dee asks.

"Of course. I wouldn't have mentioned it if I hadn't asked him first. He'll show you what to do. It's fun."

They don't hesitate. They're up and ready in a heartbeat. Dee places her flower crown on Rosie's head, just as Max knew she would, and takes her hand.

Their mom, age twelve.

How is it possible he didn't see it from the very first day, even with the Morticia hair? Her expressions, her warmth, even the tone of her voice—they're all so incredibly familiar.

There's a saying his dad likes to quote sometimes—mostly when he's annoyed with Max for doing something selfish or mean. It goes, "Give me a child until he is seven and I will show you the man." By which he basically means that Max better straighten up really soon or he runs the risk of growing up to be a jerk.

But it works the other way too: give me a girl of twelve who is warm, and kind, and clever, and generous, and I will give you the woman she grows up to be, still every one of those things.

Max is stunned by this amazing—though scary—gift of meeting his mom's younger self. Because of it, he sees her as a whole person now. Not just his take-charge mom but Dory the artist, the nature lover, the hiker, the girl who practiced being a mom when she was only twelve, because looking after Rosie gave her such a warm feeling.

It makes him love her even more.

The path along the stream is narrow, so they mostly walk in single file. Lila takes the lead, as planned, while Max sticks to Lenny, hoping for a gap in the line, a private moment to whisper, "Can we talk?"

This turns out to be unnecessary, because Lenny is on the same page. He's sticking to Max, hanging back intentionally, slowing his pace, even stopping to tie his shoe so Dee and Rosie will pass them. Now they're at the end of the line.

And then Max realizes—*of course*! Lenny wants a report on his internet search. He's dying of curiosity.

Eager to hear about his future.

"I need to tell you about a thing that's going to happen," Max says.

"I can't wait."

"It's not what you think, Lenny. It's serious."

"I die an early death?"

"No. You're just fine. But there's something you have to remember. You're really good at that, right? Remembering things?"

"Guilty as charged."

"Okay. Just so you know, this is hugely important to me. Also important for you. So listen hard."

Lenny's manner changes instantly. Max has his full attention.

"In about thirty years, you'll be in a house with another person. This house is in Edgewater, Maryland. You don't actually live there, you live in New Jersey, but you're hiding out in Maryland because you're in danger."

This literally stops him. There on the path.

"Keep walking," Max says. "You're in danger for doing something righteous, you and this other person, exposing a company that's doing bad stuff. You have the material to prove it. But the company is onto you, and they obviously don't want the information to go public. So that's why you're hiding—okay? The other person is helping you interpret the data because she knows some technical stuff you don't. So it's dangerous for both of you."

Lenny takes in a deep breath and lets it out hard. Because, yeah, this is pretty heavy stuff.

"That's just the setup. Here's the part you need to remember. Someone will come to the house. It'll be"—he does a quick calculation—"probably mid-afternoon. He'll park in front and knock on the door. Your instinct will be to hide, wait for him to go away, or maybe even sneak out the back door. Because you'll think he's the bad guys come to get you. But *don't do that*. Okay? You need to *open the door*. That's the thing I want you to remember. *Let the man in*."

"Why?"

"Because the person who's helping you? It's her husband. His name is Conrad. And he knows things you don't—about the law that protects people like you who are doing righteous things. So listen to him, okay? Do what he says."

"This is kind of astonishing."

"I'm sure it is. But it's true. So, you'll remember? You'll do what I said?"

"Yes. And yes."

"Let him in. Listen to him. Do what he says."

"Got it. Anything else?"

"Just please take this seriously."

Lenny stops again. Looks down at Max. "How on earth could I not?"

"Good."

"You know what? I'm really going to miss you."

Max is growing painfully conscious of the time. Mozelle has set her travel alarm for six thirty. When it goes off, she'll wake them up so they can finish the last of the packing and be ready when the movers arrive. And he does not want that to happen before he and Lila have said their goodbyes.

So he moves quickly. Waits till Henry has given out the assignments and everyone is starting their tasks. Henry seems almost cheerful now. He thinks that with their help he might finish the structure before the summer ends. Even the vacuum tube.

Max understands that the structure isn't real. It only exists in their collective dream. But the experience of building it, and the memory of what they created together, will change his friends in lasting ways. He's proud of bringing them all together.

Now he's stayed as long as he dares. Has said all the things you do when you're going away. Even to Dee—though he found himself, Henry-like, dropping his eyes.

Then he and Lila make their exit, to absolutely no one's surprise. His friends wave goodbye, then go back to work as they walk away.

They head straight through the woods because it's quicker and feels more private. They come out of the trees on the far side of the clearing, well beyond the playing field, and settle on a grassy slope. A good place, in the sunshine.

"So this is it," he says.

"Till next year. The campground, remember?"

He sighs. "Yeah, well, that was a great idea before I found out about Dee. No way it could happen now. It's too dangerous."

She wilts, shoulders drooping, head down, wipes her eyes with the back of her hand.

"But I have another idea. It's not awesome or fabulous, but it's something."

Her head comes up again.

"I'm going to write you a fan letter, and I'll give you my email address so you can write me back if you want."

"A fan letter for what?"

"You're going to write a book of poetry. You already have, in the real world. So I'll buy a copy and read it, then I'll write you a fan letter—a real letter, on paper, in an envelope, with a stamp on it. I'll say, you know—it's me,

Max, from back at the compound when we were twelve. And you'll write back and say, 'Of course I remember you,' and then I'll write back and tell you how things turned out with my mom. I don't care that I'll still be a kid and you'll be all grown up and married and everything. We can be pen pals. And you can sort of be my mentor. Give me wise advice."

"And if you ignore my advice and go to the dark side and end up getting arrested, I'll represent you for free."

"Well, getting arrested is not part of my life plan. And besides, I think it's already free to the client. That's the point of a public defender."

"Oh. Right."

"Don't forget to tell your dad about the records."

"I won't."

"And keep an eye on Henry. Make sure he doesn't get overwhelmed."

"Max, I can't do this. It hurts too much."

"Okay, I have a better plan."

"Another one?"

"Yes. For the rest of the time, which I don't think will be very long, let's take turns saying what we like about each other. It can be anything."

"Okay, but you can't use the posture again."

"Freckles?"

"Nope. Has to be new."

"All right. I like that you're always there, every morning, waiting for me."

"And I like that you weren't too embarrassed to hug me and cry when you were having a meltdown."

"I *was* embarrassed."

"Then I like that you did it anyway."

"Okay, I like your magical healing powers."

"I like the way you talk."

"I like the way you think."

"I like that you know about microclimates."

"I like your elastic with the plastic jewel."

"I like . . .

. . .

. . .

Chapter Nineteen

"TIME TO GET UP," Mozelle says. "Rosie's in the shower but I told her to make it quick." She walks around the bed and raises the blackout blind. Light pours into the room. "If you'd fold up the bed linens, I'd appreciate it."

When she's gone, he pulls off the pillowcase and strips the bed, folds the sheets as neatly as he can, and piles them on the bare mattress, the pillow on top. Then he sits at the end of the bed and looks around.

His mother's old room has been stripped like the bed. Her presence has been removed. The picture that hung by the door, the album full of desiccated plants, the paperbacks, and the bulldog bookends—all are packed away. Back in New York, his mom will open those boxes and remember. What and how much, Max has no idea.

He scurries out to grab some markers. Takes them back to his room. Shuts the door.

He starts by lowering the blind again. Takes the top off a red marker and writes:

THIS BLIND MADE DORY'S DREAMS
LAST LONGER
MAX'S TOO

Then he raises it again. It may be hidden, but he knows it's there.

On one side of the bed he draws his mom, age twelve. Her eyes are closed and there's a thought balloon over her head.

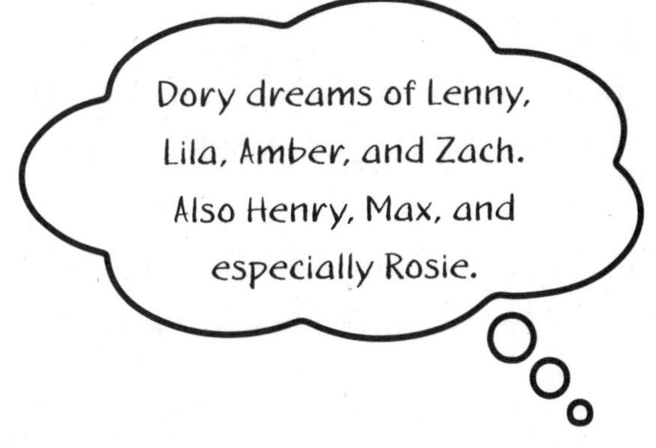

On the other side of the bed he draws himself, also with his eyes closed. In his thought balloon, which he chooses to interpret as a dream balloon, there are no words, just a picture of Lila. It's pretty crude, but it captures her spirit. He adds a bunch of hearts floating around her.

"Max?" It's Mozelle. "Rosie's out of the shower."

"Be right there!"

He doesn't have much time, but there needs to be more. Maybe just words because they don't take as long as pictures. So he quickly fills the empty white space with things his mom had done.

DORY COLLECTED PLANTS
AND PUT THEM IN A SCRAPBOOK

DORY LAY ON THIS BED
AND READ A TON OF BOOKS

DORY MADE HER OWN BOOK CALLED
THE PLANTS OF BLACKBERRY LAKE

DORY WENT DOWN TO THE STREAM
PROBABLY SHE COLLECTED ROCKS

DORY WENT OUTSIDE AT NIGHT AND GAZED AT THE STARS

"Max?" Mozelle is sounding a little frantic now, and he can finish writing his messages while the movers are loading the truck. So he goes and takes his shower. Eats his breakfast of stale banana bread, brushes his teeth, packs up his satchel, and carries it out to the car.

There's no call to Dad because he's on a plane, on his way to Baltimore. They won't hear anything for hours. He just hopes Lenny still remembers after so many years.

The truck arrives with a couple of skinny guys who look like they're in high school and this is their summer job. They're fascinated by the log cabin, which apparently they weren't expecting. But when they walk into the living room and see the literal writing on the wall, they're totally blown away.

"Dude!" one of them says. "That's so amazing!"

"We think so," Mozelle says.

"I've always wanted to do something like that."

"Feel free." She hands him a marker.

"What should I say?"

"I don't know, how about 'Dude! This is so amazing'?"

And so he does. The other driver goes with "AWESOME CABIN!"

Then they get to work carrying the couch, and tables, and the components of a queen-sized bed out the door and down the porch steps and up the ramp into the back of the U-Haul truck.

The family's only job is to stay out of their way. Max does this by going back into his bedroom and adding more activities.

DORY TAUGHT MAX AND LILA
THE RESTING STEP

DORY CROSSED THE LAKE IN A ROWBOAT

DORY MADE ROSIE A FLOWER CROWN

DORY HELPED HENRY BUILD A STRUCTURE
TO CAPTURE THE SOURCE OF THE FORCE

By ten fifteen, the movers are done. Mozelle pays them in cash. They seem exceedingly happy with what she gives them and express their sincere opinion that Mozelle is totally awesome.

Empty now, the cabin really does look like an art gallery, an open space with nothing to distract from the pictures and farewell messages on the walls. Max gets out his phone and starts clicking away, recording it all. Or not quite all, since his mom is going to see the photos, so he's very selective when he gets to the bedroom, editing out anything that has to do with the dreams.

When he's done, Mozelle pulls out her last surprise: a bag of oatmeal raisin cookies, a small pack of birthday candles, and a box of matches. "I would have preferred a cake," she says, "but we'll have to make do with cookies."

They sit in a circle on the floor while Mozelle lays three cookies out on a paper towel and presses a candle into the middle of each. They take turns lighting their candles. It feels weirdly like sitting around a campfire. Or witches cooking up a spell.

"Are we going to sing 'Happy Birthday'?" Rosie asks.

"No, I just thought we could have a moment of silence and say goodbye to the house."

"Hold on a second, though," Max says, scrambling up to take another picture. He kneels down to get it from a low angle, making sure to include lots of decorated wall in the background. Then, just to be complete, he goes back to his place in the circle, tells Mozelle and Rosie to lean in, and takes a selfie.

Mozelle tells the house goodbye, from herself and also from Marvin. Max does the same, including his mom. Rosie, with few remaining options, falls back on Fluffy Rabbit, who has not been around much lately and is currently in the car. Then they have their moment of silence and blow out their candles, and each of them writes **GOODBYE** on a wall.

"Can we eat our cookies now?"

"Absolutely."

"What about the rest of them?"

"I suggest we save them for the long drive home. Come on."

She ushers them out the back. Starts to lock the door but changes her mind. Gets Rosie in the car and starts strapping her into her booster seat.

"Um," Max says. "Before we go? One last thing?"

The seat belt clicks. Mozelle shuts Rosie's door and turns to Max, who is still standing by the kitchen door.

"What?"

"Can we please go down to the lake?"

Mozelle looks at her watch, a not-so-subtle message that she has a long drive ahead and would rather not do it in the dark.

"Seriously, when was the last time you saw it?" Max

knows the answer. She hasn't seen it in five years, maybe more. "And when do you ever expect to see it again?" He knows the answer to that one too.

"You make a very persuasive case," she says. "It's been far too long. And the lake should be part of our goodbye."

To save time, they drive to the end of the road, then park and walk down from there. He watches Mozelle's expression as she takes it all in—the rotting logs around the firepit, the missing swings, the weedy grass. "It was a lot nicer back then," she says.

"I know, but there's a place I want you to see. I promise you'll really like it."

She looks at her watch again.

"*Please*, Mozelle?"

Something in his voice makes her change her mind. "All right," she says. "As long as we're mindful of the time."

The path, at least, is unspoiled. The stream is the same. And if anything, the forest is greener, wilder, more mysterious.

"I've never been here," Mozelle says. "How marvelous."

"It's my favorite place."

"I can see why."

Max leads, picking up the pace now, because he wants

to reach Henry's clearing before they have to turn around. He knows it'll be empty, but he feels sure it will still be a holy place, a healing place, and he wants Mozelle to feel its power. He wants to feel its power too, one last time.

They've been on the path about fifteen minutes when he makes a sudden stop.

"Max," Mozelle says from behind him, "what is that?"

He just stares in silence for a long time. "It's . . . art."

"But that's not—"

"I know, Rosie. It's not the same. Come on. We have to see this up close."

It looks like an alien life-form or some bizarre creature from the depths of the sea. Woven from millions of pale, slender strips, probably bamboo, it grows like a tree from its broad base, then divides into four equal branches. They wind around one another as they arch over the water, then come together to form another base, spreading out like a flower in bloom, till it reaches the boulder in the middle of the stream, where it roots itself. Water rushes past it there, and over the lower parts of the base, but it clings firmly to the rock as if it were alive.

The source of the force.

So Henry came back, much later, in real life. Brought in all the materials. And made this incredible creation. It must have taken him forever.

"Max, that's— "

"A sculpture by Henry Rutledge, yeah."

"It's an important work! It belongs in a museum."

"No," he says. "It belongs right where it is. The sculpture is about this place. That's the reason he created it."

Rosie's walking around the base, looking for an entrance. "There's no way to get inside."

"That's not what this one's for."

Now both of them are staring at him. And since Mozelle already knows about the dreams, he figures he might as well say it. "The first one he built was to capture the power of this place directly from its source, then concentrate it so he could learn to understand it. But it never actually existed. You understand that, right? It was just part of a dream we all shared."

He's talking to Rosie now.

"I guess."

"But this"—he points to the alien life-form/undersea creature—"is real. And it's for a different purpose. Henry found out about the developer and what was going to happen here, so he wanted to protect the source before the construction started. I guess it was here all along. We just didn't know it because we only came to the clearing in our dreams, never in real life."

"Protect it how?" Rosie asks.

"Well, see how he's made a sort of loop? From the spot where his structure used to be, where the force was so strong, then over the stream and back to the boulder again. And when the force flows underground and comes back here—it's up and over and back to the rock again. It's safe, in its place. Protected."

He sees the look on Mozelle's face. "I do realize how crazy that sounds," he says. Then, following a hunch, he walks over to the sculpture. Lays a hand gently on the side of one of its branches. Waits while Mozelle and Rosie do the same.

"Can't you feel it?" he says. There's a barely audible whooshing sound, like air flowing through a duct, and a high-frequency vibration. It draws his hand to its side like a magnet, as a sensation of warmth flows up his arm and into his body. It's like listening to the best music you ever heard. Floating on a cloud. Or drifting into a perfect dream. He could stand there like that forever.

"Oh, my!" Mozelle says. "It's very strong."

He thinks about Henry coming here—by himself, or more likely with Hideo. Probably they built it together. But it must have taken months, maybe years, always during the off-season when the cabins would be empty, spring and early summer. Camping out, probably, working all day for weeks and weeks.

And he did it out of gratitude.

"I wish Marvin were here," Mozelle says. "He would have loved this so much."

"Yeah, he would."

"Thank you, Max. I'll never forget it."

"I didn't know it would be here. I thought it would be an empty clearing. But it felt important to come."

Finally Mozelle removes her hand and pulls them into a group hug. It's very sweet, and kind of sad. "I hate to leave this place," she says. "And I'll never forget it. But it's time to go home."

"Mozelle?"

"What, Rosie?"

"Can we stop at the cabin for *just a second*?"

"You need to use the bathroom?"

"No. I want to leave my cookies for the bears. On the porch, like you said."

"Well, gosh. I can't see that it would do any harm now."

"Because they're so shy and they never bothered us. And I think we should do something nice for them too."

"You know, Rosie, I think that's exactly what we should do."

"Good."

"And then we'll go home."

Chapter Twenty

Dear Lila,

A long time ago (for you, not for me) I promised to read your book of poems, then write you a fan letter. This is me doing that. Actually, it's a whole lot more than just a fan letter, but I'll start with the book—which is awesome, and not just because I'm in it.

I've thought a lot about what you wrote, especially the "collective mythology" thing. It feels very true, the way we created something so totally amazing with our minds all working together. But it's also amazing how our "mind-meld" (excuse the nerdy Star Trek reference—I couldn't resist!)

somehow made us all a little bit more of what we were meant to be. I know it changed me a lot.

So—I know how your life turned out because, as I told you, I looked it up. I'm glad it's been good. You're doing important stuff, helping people and changing lives. None of that surprises me. You were always a star. Then you became bold. :-)

Now for the update. Thanks to you (and also to me) (and also a data guru named Marcus) my dad found where Mom and Lenny were hiding. Well, you know that already because I told you, but not what happened later.

Our whistleblower theory was right. I told you about Lenny's job at the big drug company, remember? He was in charge of all the data—and by that I mean everything. But, Lenny being Lenny, with his famous photographic memory (which he denies even exists but I still don't believe him) didn't just manage all that data. He read it. Better still, he read it and remembered it.

So when he was going through all these documents on this one big super-bestselling drug and noticed that, somewhere along the way, the numbers had changed and some inconvenient stuff had magically disappeared from one of the studies—well, naturally he looked into it. And the more he looked the more he found. Not just that drug. Others, too.

So he started downloading evidence onto thumb drives

and sneaking them though security at the end of the day and storing them in a safe deposit box. It's like something out of a movie.

Then he took a week of vacation and drove up to the Finger Lakes with his laptop and all the thumb drives to do some serious, uninterrupted research. Two days later he got a call from a neighbor who was keeping an eye on his house while he was gone. She said she'd seen some "suspicious activity"—people moving around inside the house with flashlights, a bunch of them, at like three in the morning—so she called the police. Maybe the bad guys had a police scanner or something, because they were gone before the cops arrived. They'd taken Lenny's big computer and all the files in his office but left a lot of valuable things. The police said it didn't look like a normal burglary. They were clearly looking for something in particular.

That's what Lenny thought, too. It sounded like Lauette security was onto him, which meant he was in danger of who knew what. So he bought the burner phone, drove to Newark Airport, and left his car in long-term parking with his real phone in the glove compartment. I guess he hoped the security people would think he'd run off to Brazil or something. Anyway, that's when he called Mom. And when she got there, they took the train to Baltimore and rented a car.

Sorry this is so long, but you have to admit it's pretty

exciting stuff. And you were a big part of helping Mom and Lenny, so I thought you'd like to know.

Anyway, as I told you way back then, there's this really fine line between taking confidential data for the purpose of exposing fraud and taking that data and handing it over to some reporter at the *Washington Post*. Well, you're a lawyer, so that probably makes sense to you. I don't really understand it myself. But if Lenny had handled it the wrong way, things could have gone really badly for him.

So Dad went down there to Maryland and told him what he needed to do (and not do!) so he could get the bad guys without going to prison. They drove up to Pennsylvania to meet with this famous lawyer who specializes in whistleblower cases. Over and out to them.

Meanwhile, Lenny can go wherever he wants. If the lawyers need to interview him, or ask questions, they'll go to him. Which is good, since he no longer has a job and his money will go a lot farther in Mexico. Once the story breaks, he'll be a hero.

Mom is fine, but I think the whole thing was kind of scary for her. Like the security guys were tailing them, and they had some really close calls, and then later it looked like maybe they'd found the house in Maryland, because someone seemed to be watching them. She and Lenny were trying to figure out a way to get out without being seen, probably late at night, when (thanks to us) Dad arrived and (also thanks to us) Lenny let him in.

Mom and I had a long talk, like you said we should, once everything was over. I "unpacked" a lot of stuff, probably too much, about what she put us through, and how we were just kids, and Rosie was such a mess back then, and poor Mozelle, and poor Dad. She cried and so did I. But weirdly, I came out of it better than when we started. I don't just mean I *feel* better now because I let all that anger out. I mean I'm better as a person, more forgiving and not as selfish. Because I got to see the whole thing from Mom's point of view, and how hard it was for her to make that choice, but it was the right one, and she and Lenny may have saved a lot of people from harm. I learned some other stuff too. I'm still thinking about it.

One thing we didn't talk about, and probably never will, was the dreaming. And Dad's in on it too, I'm pretty sure, because he has weirdly never asked me how I knew about Lenny. I mean, he asked when I first called him, and I just said it was complicated, but after that he never mentioned it again. So he definitely knows something, not sure what. And of course Mozelle knows too. So I guess what we've got now is one big family conspiracy of silence. Which is okay, and definitely easier. And it all had a happy ending.

Meanwhile, I have my book, which I'm still working on. And

my memories. And maybe also, every now and then, a letter or email from you.

One last thing. It's my way of saying thanks for being so important in my life, even if it was just for a week. And it's a really, really awesome gift. So here it is:

This weekend, you and your family need to get in your car and go to the compound. Yeah, I know, it's a really long drive from Boston! I looked it up on a map. But do it anyway. And you need to go there now, before all the noise and destruction starts. And while your cabin's still there, so you can show it to your kids. You can even go inside. (I left the back door unlocked.)

After that, go to Henry's clearing. If you don't remember how to get there, just cross the playing field and keep on going till you reach the stream. Turn right and follow the path into the woods, about fifteen minutes. Then you'll see it, my gift. Henry's gift. Stay as long as you can.

You're welcome.

Your old friend,
Max Sotelo
max.sotelo8876@gmail.com

About the Author

DIANE STANLEY is the author and illustrator of beloved books for young readers, including *The Silver Bowl*, named a best book of the year by *Kirkus Reviews* and an ALA *Booklist* Editors' Choice; *The Cup and the Crown*; *The Princess of Cortova*; *Saving Sky*, winner of the Arab American Book Award; *Bella at Midnight*, a *School Library Journal* Best Book of the Year and an ALA *Booklist* Editors' Choice; *The Mysterious Case of the Allbright Academy*; *The Mysterious Matter of I. M. Fine*; *The Chosen Prince*; and *Joplin, Wishing*. Ms. Stanley has written and illustrated numerous picture books, including three creatively reimagined fairy tales, *The Giant and the Beanstalk*, *Goldie and the Three Bears*, and *Rumpelstiltskin's Daughter*, and an award-winning series of picture book biographies. She lives in Santa Fe, New Mexico. You can visit her online at www.dianestanley.com.